D1109392

WITHDRAWN

BAC SI

A NOVEL

TOM BELLINO

outskirtspress
DENVER, COLORADO

This is a work of fiction. The events and characters described herein are imaginary and are not intended to refer to specific places or living persons. The opinions expressed in this manuscript are solely the opinions of the author and do not represent the opinions or thoughts of the publisher. The author has represented and warranted full ownership and/or legal right to publish all the materials in this book.

Bac Si
A Novel
All Rights Reserved.
Copyright © 2015 Tom Bellino
v3.0

Cover Photo © 2015 Unknown Vietnamese artist. All rights reserved - used with permission.

This book may not be reproduced, transmitted, or stored in whole or in part by any means, including graphic, electronic, or mechanical without the express written consent of the publisher except in the case of brief quotations embodied in critical articles and reviews.

Outskirts Press, Inc.
http://www.outskirtspress.com

Paperback ISBN: 978-1-4787-5105-2
Hardback ISBN: 978-1-4787-5221-9

Outskirts Press and the "OP" logo are trademarks belonging to Outskirts Press, Inc.

PRINTED IN THE UNITED STATES OF AMERICA

DEDICATION

For the Veterans of that place and time we call Viet Nam.

For my mother and my daughters, and for their encouragement to write this story.

"Got in a little hometown jam.
So they put a rifle in my hand.
Sent me off to a foreign land.
To go and kill the yellow man."

Bruce Springsteen
"Born in the U.S.A."

"If you were there, I don't need to explain.
If you weren't, I can't explain."

James Webb
Former Secretary of the Navy,
Virginia Senator, and
Viet Nam War veteran
CBS Sunday Morning,
May 25, 2014

"Once upon a time, a girl with moonlight in her eyes,
put her hand in mine, and said she loved me so.
But that was once upon a time, very long ago."

Tony Bennett
"Once upon a time."

PROLOGUE

The mind is a wondrous place. It holds memories, pleasant ones and painful ones. These memories may surface unexpectedly, or when its master, the mind, conjures them up. The definition of memory is the retention of learned experiences. There are two types of memories, primary or short term, and secondary or long term. The former endures for a very brief period of time. The latter reflects the knowledge of a former state of mind after it has already once dropped from consciousness. We should be thankful for both.

So let it be with the memories of war, and so let it be with the memories of innocent love. These experiences are, or should be retained in our memories lest we not learn from our experiences, the ones that brought us pleasure as well as pain.

The mid 1960's are years typical of that yin and yang of the memory process. It was during those years that many happy and many painful memories were forged for a generation. They still linger today. What one does with those memories, the good ones and the bad ones, characterizes this story.

CHAPTER 1

Her almond shaped eyes looked up at me when she said, "Xin chao, Bac Si," which I knew was Vietnamese for "Hello Doctor."

"Xin chao, Quynh. You look very pretty this morning. Did you have breakfast?"

"Oh yes, Bac Si. Cam on (thank you)."

"English, Quynh, remember?" This little 8-year-old girl took my hand and we walked down the long, gray and blue hall, to my office, where she sat on the chair next to my desk, in her little dark blue pleated skirt with a white, navy style jumper top, ever so prim and proper. Her pitch black hair was cut in a typical Asian, little girl style, with bangs to her mid forehead. After she sat there for a couple of minutes, she looked at me, and politely picked up one of the crayons on the desk and began drawing. She knew the routine, as she had been doing it since she was first assigned to my service, Pediatric Neuropsychology, two months before.

Typically on this service, the focus was on the assessment and treatment of brain disorders, usually resulting from either physical trauma or any syndrome, such as autism or even Attention Deficit Disorder. In Quynh's case, she initially presented with mutism, an inability to speak. The question asked by her neurologist was whether this mutism, which had a relatively sudden onset, was a function of some brain dysfunction of a clearly physical nature, even though nothing showed up on scans, or was this some sudden onset psychological issue, which would later be classified as post-traumatic stress disorder. It took only four sessions for Quynh to begin to talk, and speak to me, but that was only after I had placed crayons and paper in front of her, as I drew some pictures with another set of crayons and paper on my side of the desk. And, once she started talking, she could not stop. So much for mutism. But later, a clear, post- traumatic stress disorder became manifested. She came to describe her dreams and nightmares with such detail that I could almost see them myself. And when she did describe them, she became either acutely anxious and agitated, or quietly depressed. When either of those symptoms occurred, she would grasp my hand and squeeze it so tightly that she would leave her little finger indentations on my hand or wrist, and frequently on both.

Actually she did not want to sit directly across from me, as other children I saw in treatment did, but rather at the side of the desk. In the first few sessions she merely looked up at me, and then down at the pictures I was drawing. I drew some scenes with trees and birds. Clearly I was not an artist, and once Quynh even laughed when I tried to draw a dog. It was then that she picked up a crayon and began to doodle. Then she drew. She always started with the green crayon, and then proceeded to the red one and then the black one. She drew large, green palm fronds that covered virtually the entire page. It was clear that what she was drawing was the jungle. There was a small structure in her drawing, which she described as her house, her home in Viet Nam. The roof was the beige color of weathered bamboo, and was clearly thatched. The walls were clearly of bamboo, but darker than the roof, and they had large sections of red. When I asked her about the red part of the house she looked down and bit her lip. She shook her head, so we didn't go there. I was sure I knew what the red on the top and sides of the house represented, but I certainly didn't want to feed her symptoms, especially if I was wrong, and merely projecting something from my own background, or even something I might have seen in a movie or television show.

Quynh really was such a polite little girl, and I was confident that she was developing a trust in me. Perhaps it was because I would attempt to talk with her in her native language, which I was trying to learn. I had purchased all the Vietnamese language tapes I could, and was actually proceeding through the second level of a three level program of that language. I always had a knack for languages, and had mastered several, including Italian and French. But, in Quynh's case, not only was Vietnamese her native language, but so was French, which was a function of her being educated early in her young life by French speaking nuns. So, "bon jour" was just as likely to come out of her mouth as was good morning. I had learned French in college, and then had to perfect it, as if any non-Frenchman could ever perfect French, as a requirement for the Masters Degree. German was the language I had to learn, to some extent, for the Ph.D. requirement. I didn't master that guttural language, and had difficulty in keeping straight the der, die, das, die, which are the German articles for the word "the." I found German a difficult language, but yet I was able to study and learn Vietnamese, in spite of the almost guttural quality of that language as well. Perhaps it was because I was through with academic requirements, that Vietnamese was easier to master than was German, and in working with Quynh, I was happy that I learned, or at least was learning Vietnamese. Little did I know, or realize, that studying this language would propel me into a bittersweet part of my life, less than 24 months in the future. And in the shelter of Bethesda, I had no idea yet, what the 1000-yard stare was.

"Bac Si, I like to draw with these crayons, but I am not sure you like what I draw."

"Why do you say that, Quynh?"

"Because you always lean forward when I use the green crayon, and then you really lean forward when I use the red one, but not so much with the black one."

I didn't realize that I was giving that "tell" but I couldn't deny that I was doing it and that it probably was noticeable to this bright little girl.

"Well Little One, I have to admit, you are probably right and I think I will tell you why. I think something happened to your house in Viet Nam, and that you saw it happen. Can you tell me about it?"

"I miss my house, Bac Si, and I think about it beaucoup. I think my brother is still there, but I am not sure. I know I saw him run away."

"Can you tell me about it honey?"

"I don't want to talk about it today Bac Si. Is that ok? Will you be sad if I don't want to talk about it today?"

"No little one, I won't be sad. You can talk about it if and when you want to, hieu (understand)? But, we have to stop for today. Commander and Mrs. Mason are waiting for you in the waiting room. I will see you next week, OK?"

"Vang (Yes) Bac Si. Tam biet (Goodbye) Bac Si. I like talking with you."

That sweet little girl took my hand as I walked her out to the waiting room where her adopting parents, Commander and Mrs. William Mason, were waiting for her, and were smiling as she ran to them and hugged them both. She tried to wrap her little arms around both of them at the same time. It was obvious that Quynh loved them and felt so secure with them. And, it was apparent that the Commander and his wife loved this eight year old little girl, and would do anything to assuage the psychic pain they knew she must still have after all that they knew she went through in Viet Nam, before they were able to get her out through a Catholic child relief organization, in Saigon. They learned all about her village being burned down by the Viet Cong because the guerillas thought the village was cooperating with the enemy, the soldiers of the United States. The Viet Cong burned the village, including Quynh's house, and killed her parents and sister, and chased into the jungle her brother, Tran, who was eight years Quynh's senior. She was able to escape only by hiding in a well a hundred meters from the village, while she was going to get some water and had heard the gunfire and screaming coming from her village. She did not recognize the voices of the screaming people, but knew about how the Viet Cong burned homes and killed villagers from nearby areas. And, it was ironic that her brother was sympathetic to Hanoi, and North Viet Nam, but was still so frightened that he had to run. However, his ideas were formed as he learned in school that the French tried to colonize his country, and that now, he was convinced that the Americans were trying to do the same. She remembered how Tran came home from school one day so angry because he learned that in spite of a victory for the Vietnamese, so many of his countrymen were killed by the French, at Diem Bien Phu, including an uncle whose picture was proudly displayed by his parents, in their home. Quynh loved her brother and described a very close relationship with him. She confided that when food was scarce, Tran would somehow get her a little more rice because she was hungry and she would tell him so. The only items that she was able to carry with her from Viet Nam were a small picture of her family, her father, mother, sister, Tran and her, and another one of Tran wearing a "non la," which is the traditional conical hat made usually of palm leaf.

CHAPTER 2

Four Years Earlier
Marquette University Campus

"**H**i, are you going to Norge Village?"
What a way to try to pick up a good looking young coed, but she really was good looking and I really wanted to meet her, so I had to say something.

Norge Village was a laundromat on Wells Street, right off campus, where students took their laundry to either wash or have dry-cleaned. The reason it was called Norge Village is because all of the machines, washers and dryers, were made by Norge. It was also a student's restaurant area that years later would be the hunting grounds of Jeffrey Daumer, where he would eat people. Besides the smell of hops in the air from the breweries, around the Laundromat you could always smell the exhaust from the dryers. But in this case I thought I smelled this pretty young girl's perfume, or maybe it was her soap. But, whatever it was, she was perhaps the most beautiful girl I had ever seen, and seeing her was a fortuitous accident. Oh, I had seen and gone out with many girls since I had been at Marquette, but none had completely knocked my socks off, as did the sight of this girl.

She turned around and smiled and said, " Do I look like I need to go to Norge Village?"

At least she didn't just keep walking and ignore me, like I feared she might do.

"Cute," I said, "both that, and you."

She smiled the most beautiful smile I had ever seen, and walked back to me and said, "Thanks, and that was good."

I was a Psychology major, with a Modern Language minor. I debated trying to dazzle her with something in French or Italian, but I thought better of it, since it looked like I was on a roll in English. We chatted for a few minutes, mostly about school, our majors, the weather. I asked her if I could walk with her for a bit, and she said that her dorm was just a couple of blocks away, and that yes, that would be great.

I introduced myself to her, by sticking out my hand and said, "I'm Tommy Staffieri, what's your name?"

She introduced herself to me by taking my hand in both of hers and said, "Hi, my name is Carolyn Young."

Her handshake had the firm and vigorous qualities I would associate with someone who was raised on a farm, and as it turned out, she had, in fact, been raised on a farm, in South Dakota, near Rapid City. Yet, she was unmistakably feminine. She had the most beautiful eyes, and even though she was wearing a long sweater, I could tell she had a great figure. Her smile was captivating. Little did I realize then, that I would be carrying this encounter with me half way around the world, and half way through my life.

Maybe it was her beauty. Maybe it was the sweetness of her voice. Maybe it was, well everything about her. All I knew at that moment was that I wanted this to last forever. So, I asked her out, and she said yes. And I asked her out again, and again, and she kept saying yes. I don't think that I had ever been so happy. And, we continued to go out, regularly, and both of us were so happy.

We dated exclusively, and although like so many college romances, some things, like jealousy, probably more on my part, got in the way, nothing diminished what both of us knew we had, something special. And, we never argued, about anything. I took her to fraternity parties,

concerts, and basketball games. We went to some of the better restaurants in Milwaukee, like Mader's, but we also went to the dives to
have pizza and listen to music. We had a great time no matter where
we went. We laughed, we sang, we talked, we planned, and we kissed.
We also attended church together every Sunday, and held hands during the Mass. And sometimes during Mass, we would draw letters in
each other's palms with our fingers, spelling out "I love you." We had
a great love life, and the sex was incredible. And it wasn't just sex, it
was lovemaking.

Although for probably the first time in my life I was actually pay-
ing attention to my studies, and my grades were showing it. We even
studied together. Maybe it was because with her, I was really feeling
content. We were getting so close, both emotionally and physically. I
was feeling that not only was she the most beautiful girl I ever met,
but also the smartest. In my eyes she could do no wrong. I was really
smitten. I kept wanting to be so deep inside of her, that she was all I
could think about. The first time we really went at it and making out,
we were parked in front of her dorm. She was wearing this beautiful
silver-gray dress, which she later told me she had made it herself. As
I moved in for the feel, second base, in my clearly uncertain way I
asked her, "Do you want me to?" She nodded yes, and I was in heaven.
We progressed over the months to the best love making in my life. We
spent as much time together as we could. We would meet in the student union between classes, for coffee. We even actually took a couple
of classes together, just so we could be together. After several months,
we had even become "pinned." By me giving her my fraternity pin,
that was sort of being "engaged to be engaged." My fraternity brothers
even serenaded us in front of her dorm, the weekend after the pinning.
They presented her with a bouquet of roses. Everything was perfect.
She was truly an angel.

But then reality reared its head. It was the middle of May. I knew
that I had to leave. We both knew it. Graduation. I was so looking

forward to that day, yet dreading it because I knew I would have to leave this angel behind. Actually, we both had to leave, even though she still had another year to go before she would graduate. She sat with my mother at the graduation ceremony, and afterwards we did the family celebration lunch. The three of us, my mother, Carolyn, and I, laughed, reminisced, and even talked about the future, but when we discussed the future, Carolyn began to tear up. Then so did my mother. So did I.

Later, Carolyn and I walked the campus, and even made a point of walking by Norge Village, where it all began. Where we began.

On the night before I left, we walked along the War Memorial, on the Milwaukee Lakefront, hand in hand, and not saying a whole heck of a lot. I guess we both feared that something beautiful was ending; and hoping it wouldn't end.

She pulled me close and said, "Tommy, I love you. Please don't ever forget me. I will never forget you. You are the love of my life. I know you have to go. Can I go with you? I will quit school if you will take me with you. Oh Tommy, do you think we will ever see each other again? I can't bear to think that we will not be together."

She had tears in her eyes, as did I. I held her so close, and wanted to be so deep inside of her one more time. God I loved this girl. How could I ever forget her? I even thought that maybe I should ask her to quit school and come with me to Washington, and that she could finish there, either at Georgetown or at Catholic University of America. Ultimately though, I knew that that probably would not be a good idea, either for her or for me.

She brought some pictures of her I had not seen before. They were of her holding a pet fox, back in South Dakota. She was so beautiful in those pictures, and she still looked the same. She was just so lovely as I stared at her, tears streaming down her face.

I held those pictures close to my heart and said, "Carolyn, wherever I am, wherever I go, you will always be with me. I promise you that you are the love of my life."

As I took her back to her dorm, and we hugged so tight, not saying a word, we had said it all. We professed our love, although we had done that all the times we made love all that year. She kissed me so hard, and put my hand on her right breast, the "Do you want me to?" breast. And then she turned around and ran into the dorm. I could hear her sobbing as she ran. And, that is when I, too, started sobbing, covering my eyes with my hands. I was walking away from the love of my life. But I had to. My calling was calling. I knew I had to go to graduate school and not just to avoid the draft. I really wanted to become a psychologist. I had been accepted into the Clinical Psychology Program, at Georgetown University, in Washington, D.C. I was initially torn between Clinical Psychology and Modern Languages, and actually had applied to both programs and had been accepted by both, and had even thought I could do both. But I also knew that whichever path I chose, I would carry her pictures with me, wherever I went, and that maybe some day............

CHAPTER 3

Neuropsychology Unit
Bethesda Naval Hospital
5 January 1969

"Dr. Staffieri, you have 5 patients today, including a screening for Operation Deep Freeze, and your last patient is your favorite, little Quynh, and then you have a meeting with Captain Mullins, the Chief of Psychiatry, as well as the Medical Director of the hospital, at 1600, and I know you don't want to miss that."

"Thanks Sybil, and if Lieutenant Richards calls or comes by, let me know right away, ok?"

Navy Lieutenant Cheryl Richards was the Navy nurse I met when I first arrived at Bethesda. When I met her on the elevator, in Building Seven, I recognized her from the psych unit, where as interns, we rounded with the psychiatry residents and attendings. She was tall, and had raven hair, with a little white streak along the side. And, in addition to her obvious movie starlet looks, she had great legs. And, she had actually started the conversation with me. That surprised me because I am usually the one who comes on to pretty girls, and Cheryl was great looking, and her Navy nurses uniform made her even more attractive. She did outrank me, since I was actually a LTJG, a Lieutenant Junior Grade, and she was a full Lieutenant. I knew I would be making full Lieutenant any day now, and certainly by the time I finished the internship year. Maybe that was what Sybil was trying to suggest to me when she said that I wouldn't want to miss the appointment with Captain Mullins.

Sybil Sheradin was the unit secretary, but actually she was a sort of major domo. She ran the place. If you needed any new testing material, a book, or some equipment that you thought was un-gettable, she would somehow come up with it. And, she knew everyone and everything about everyone in the hospital. And, she knew about promotions even before they happened. So, maybe she knew something about mine. Maybe I would be making full Lieutenant before my internship was over. That would be great, since it would mean more money to send home to "mamma," and to help pay off my graduate school loans. I had won different fellowships, but none of them quite covered my expenses, especially since my mother, back in Gary, Indiana, really depended on me to supplement her social security and her pension from U.S. Steel, where she worked as a laborer for over thirty years. She was a "single mother" before it became somewhat fashionable to claim single mother status.

A promotion this soon into the internship year would definitely be unusual, so Captain Walter Mullins, Medical Corps, United States Navy, Chief of Psychiatry, National Naval Medical Center, Bethesda Naval Hospital, probably had something else to talk with me about. He knew I was interested in the "Operation Deep Freeze" at McMurdo Station, in Antarctica, evaluation program, in addition to my pediatric specialty. I was interested in stress, and its impact on children, but also found the effects of stress, both from combat as well as isolation an interesting phenomenon. The guys, there were no women in the program yet, who were being considered for the Operation Deep Freeze program were volunteers, who would be going for year long tour in Antarctica. I simply couldn't imagine anyone wanting to do that or go there. Yet, these young men, from eighteen to twenty-five, actually wanted to go down there. It was my job to evaluate their suitability to handle such a remote and isolated existence. I was really learning a lot in my internship, and I found myself coming in early and staying late in the hospital. I found the Bethesda Naval Hospital an exciting place. There was always something interesting going on, and I found myself going to psychiatric rounds, neurology rounds, and neurosurgery rounds. I simply could not get enough of what I was seeing at The National Naval Medical Center. Even listening to the "yellow berets," the doctors from the Public Health Service, which was located across the street from the Naval Hospital, on Wisconsin Avenue, at the National Institutes of Health, was something I looked forward to, when they gave seminars to their Navy counterparts at Bethesda.

CHAPTER 4

Captain Mullins' Office

"Come in Lieutenant."

"Yes sir. Lieutenant Thomas Staffieri reporting as ordered, sir."

"At ease Lieutenant. Admiral Johnson, the Medical Director of the Hospital, couldn't make it today, so it will be only the two of us. How do you like your internship? How do you like the Navy?"

"Fine Sir, thank you. I like them both."

"Captain Flaherty, your Chief of Navy Psychology, tells me that you are doing an outstanding job in the clinic, and you are staying late and seeing more patients and doing more evaluations than required. May I ask why?"

"Well Sir, after graduate school, and externship at D.C. General, I feel that I am truly making a difference with my work here, and I really like what I am doing."

"I know it is a bit premature, Lieutenant, but have you thought of making the Navy a career? You could be on a fast track to leadership in Navy Psychology. And, with your language skills, well who knows where that might take you."

I was thinking that my interest in languages was not really a well known thing, but I suppose with the Viet Nam War in full swing, and the Tet Offensive being in the news, that my interest in Vietnamese probably made some rounds, especially when talk about the "gooks" became heated.

"Yes Sir, I had initially spoken with Captain Flaherty, when he first recruited me for the internship program, about the possibility of a subsequent tour in Gaeta, Italy, which would be great, since my family is from not too far from there, near L'Aquila, in the Abruzzi, northeast of Rome."

"You speak Italian, do you Lieutenant? Among other languages, I understand? Five, isn't it? Italian, French, Portuguese, Spanish, and now Vietnamese?"

"Yes Sir. I was lucky enough to grow up in Gary, Indiana, where if you couldn't converse and do business in a number of languages, you couldn't get along. Gary was, and is, a very ethnic city. And besides, I have always liked languages."

"Lieutenant, I would like for you to have lunch with me next week, and we can explore your Navy options, but in the meantime I have a couple of matters I have to present you with immediately. First of all, congratulations, you have been promoted to full Lieutenant, as of today. I have your promotion papers here on my desk. They were sent over today, from the Bureau of Personnel, BuPers. Clearly you were on a fast track for this promotion. Congratulations Lieutenant."

"Thank you very much Sir." Captain Mullins shook my hand and called the Naval Hospital photographer to come in and take the picture of him shaking my hand and presenting me with my Lieutenant bars. After that brief ceremony, I thought we were finished, and started edging towards the door.

"One more thing Lieutenant, I have your orders for when you complete your internship in June. Would you care to read them or would you like me to tell you where the Navy is sending you? Where the Navy needs you."

"Please tell me, Sir. I am so surprised about the promotion that reading the orders might not sink in. Just please don't tell me that I am going to go to McMurdo, for Operation Deep Freeze. Although I admire the young men who volunteer to go down there sir, but frankly, I went to school in Milwaukee, and that was cold enough for me." We both laughed. "Sir, although that would not be my first choice for my next duty station, or even my second or third choice, you know that I will do or go where ever I need to go." As I said that, I thought I sounded like, at least to myself, a kiss-ass. I hoped I wasn't sounding like one to the Captain. He laughed again, and I felt a bit relieved, but still waited for him to tell me. Would it be Naval Hospital, Long Beach? Would it be Great Lakes, in Chicago, which would be close to my hometown? I would love to teach at the Naval Academy, in Annapolis, and that would be close to "Mother Bethesda." Would I be staying at Bethesda? No, they wouldn't keep me here, since Bethesda would be a senior billet, which means a Commander or at least a Lieutenant Commander.

"Lieutenant you have been assigned to..........."

CHAPTER 5

Neuropsychology Unit

"The Repose? THE Repose? The Hospital Ship? That's unbelievable. You are going to war. You're going to friggin' war, and you don't even know how to shoot a gun. But at least you will be in the South China Sea, far enough away from the action in-country, in Viet Nam, that the gooks won't get you, and the Navy nurses are supposed to be great......great looking that is."

"Stop it George, and let me digest this. This isn't at all what I expected. The caveat, however, is that I get to spend three months at the Mental Health Clinic, Pearl Harbor Shipyard, before I have to report to the Repose. I am going to help relieve the patient backlog at the clinic until they can get another psychiatrist there. Seems as though there are a number of Marines coming back from Nam who 'can't take it anymore,' and want out before their enlistment is up."

Lieutenant Junior Grade George Chase was my fellow intern, and close friend. We came on board at Bethesda at the same time, and started our internship on the same day. We bonded immediately, even though he was somewhat patrician, from Boston, and tried to make fun of me coming from "the region," which was short for The Calumet Region, which meant Gary, Indiana.

Smirking he said "You can always use your switchblade if you see any combat. I'm sure all you 'region rats' have your switchblades, right?"

"Some of our mayors might have gone to prison, George, but not all of us from Gary are criminals, nor are the Italians there all 'connected'." That was another of George's obsessions, that all Italians must have some mafia ties, and hence 'connected.' Of course I didn't help my case any by frequently referring to him as the 'strunz from Boston." It wasn't until a month into our training that I told him that a 'strunz' or actually 'stronzo' was Italian for turd. But in spite of our mutual teasing, we developed a good friendship, based on professional and personal respect and concern.

Actually, George was the only person I had ever told about Carolyn, the love of my life, from Marquette. The one I left behind, yet could not forget. I guess until then I just didn't want to share that part of my heart with anyone. And George was not only sympathetic, but he was a good psychologist. He knew how to listen. He also could be directive and advice giving. We explored the options of trying to contact Carolyn. He was happily married, having married the love of HIS life in graduate school, right after he finished his Masters, and right before he started on his Ph.D. He encouraged me to try to contact Carolyn, but those were the days before Google and the Internet, and perhaps more importantly, I just didn't want to open up a wound in my heart, and possibly Carolyn's, which I just didn't know I could close. Too much time had passed. I had too much that I still had to do, and so many places I knew I would have to go. I did know, however, that I still had Carolyn's pictures with me, and that the memory of her was tucked away in my heart. That would never change. I had no idea the extent to which that never changing would be.....or how far away I would eventually take those pictures.

CHAPTER 6

Bethesda Naval Hospital

My internship year at Bethesda Naval Hospital was, all things considered, one of the happiest years of my life. As a Naval Officer I made more money than I had ever made in my life. Perhaps that wasn't saying much inasmuch as I had been a graduate student for three years, and before that, four years as an undergraduate. Well actually 5 years as an undergraduate. I was a "super senior," since I had actually transferred to Marquette, from Indiana University, where I was on the baseball team, but promptly flunked out, in spite of "tutor table." Our family doctor, a graduate of Marquette, encouraged me and helped facilitate my acceptance and transfer to Marquette. But, I had to make up the Theology and Philosophy requirements for a Marquette degree in Liberal Arts, regardless of major field of study.

The Jesuits, at Marquette, quickly turned me around academically, and put me on the path to at least a modicum of academic success, enough so that I was accepted into graduate school at Georgetown, with a substantial fellowship. The Clinical Psychology program there was outstanding and had arrangements for their students to do externships, or placements, at St. Elizabeth's, which was famous for the severity of mental illness of their patients. Also, D.C. General served as a training ground for treating some of the more disturbed patients from the District of Columbia. With those types of experiences, Internships at leading hospitals and centers around the country were happy to

accept all five of my Psychology program class. We had started with
seven, but two didn't make it through the doctoral preliminary exams
after the Masters Degree. With the Viet Nam War raging, and the un-
popularity of that war at many universities, my professors as well as
fellow students were surprised that I interviewed with the Director of
Clinical Training at Bethesda Naval Hospital, definitely a military program. There were two options at Bethesda, I found out about. One, I
could come in as a civilian, or I could apply for a commission as a Naval
Officer in the Medical Service Corps, and then would owe the Navy
two more years after the internship. I had already received a "greeting"
from the Draft Board back in Gary, but was able to get a deferment
while I was still in school, especially since it was a health related program. The "greeting," I had received started out with "Greeting. Your
friends and neighbors have selected you........" I thought, "wow, some
friends and neighbors." I knew that I would be receiving another, and
probably my final "greeting," and this one ordering me to Army boot
camp. Although if I were drafted I would probably be sent to officer's
training. I had heard the horror stories that the life expectancy of a
Second Lieutenant in Viet Nam, being seven seconds. But, that is not
what made me interview and ultimately apply to the Navy Clinical
Psychology Internship Program. I felt that there was something going
on in the world, and that I needed to be a part of it. My country needed me I thought, albeit perhaps somewhat grandiosely, and besides
that the pay was good. The program that was described both by the director as well as the literature, was interesting and sounded stimulat-
ing, and I was also assured that my interest in languages would clearly
be considered in any possible career track should I opt to stay in the
Navy, as a career Navy Psychologist. Possible duty stations like Pearl
Harbor, Naples, Italy, the Naval Academy, were all mentioned, and
of course I thought that that possibility was too good to pass up. So I
signed up. I received my orders to report to one of the Old Navy buildings on Constitution Avenue, not far from the White House. There, I

was sworn in and commissioned as an Ensign, and immediately promoted to Lieutenant Junior Grade, LTJG. I was disbursed a check in the amount of three hundred dollars for my uniform allowance, and directed back to the National Naval Medical Center, Bethesda Naval Hospital, Department of Psychology. I met with Dr. Ike Samuelson, the director of Clinical Training, Miss Elizabeth Hanson, the Chairperson of Clinical Training, who was actually the world's foremost authority on the Rorschach Inkblot Test as well as other projective personality tests. And, the Chief of Navy Psychology, Captain William Flaherty was also there to greet me. After we had our welcoming session in the Psychology Department, Captain Flaherty took me to the office of Captain Mullins, in the Psychiatry wing of the hospital rather than the administrative office. Captain Flaherty was the person who had actually recruited me into the program. He was a close friend of my major professor at Georgetown. Inasmuch as I was not yet in uniform, I felt a bit uncomfortable, but everyone made me feel welcomed and gradually I felt that I belonged. After the meeting, Sybil walked me over to the uniform shop in the Base Exchange, and told them to give me what I needed. I handed over my uniform allotment check and said, "Just give me everything that I need that this check will buy." So much for my boot camp. A direct commission in the Psychology Program of the Medical Service Corps, was exactly that, a direct commission. There was no basic training, no instruction on how to wear the uniform, or even what uniform and rank insignias to have. I relied solely on the wisdom and goodness of the people in the uniform shop. They must have realized my predicament, and said that they would have the uniforms altered and ready for me the next day, and promised me that they would show me how to put on the shoulder boards, insignias, and even tell me who to salute. It was a month later that I was ordered to the Naval School of Hospital Administration, on the Bethesda campus, where I would spend the next thirty days learning about the Navy, its history, mission, and how to wear the uniform. And, we were all encouraged to ditch any "love beads" we might be wearing as a carry over from "hippie days in school." I kept mine, and wore them under my uniform. They were somewhat covered by my dog tags. That was my rebellion against uniformity and also a way to maintain my link to studentness. I guess I was probably the Navy Medical Service Corps version of the rebellious "Hawkeye Pierce," the Army doctor played by Alan Alda in the movie M.A.S.H. (Mobile Army Surgical Hospital).

The two things I carried throughout my Navy career were those love beads and those pictures of that special coed from years ago.

CHAPTER 7

In Transit

Leaving the cocoon of "Mother Bethesda" was difficult. That internship year truly was one of the best years of my life. And now, I was a newly minted psychologist, a naval officer, and I had a goal, a purpose, and money in my pocket. But leaving the comfort of what I knew, as well as the great people I met, including Cheryl, the Navy nurse, who was really one of the sweetest people I had ever met, was difficult for me. Cheryl and I spent a lot of time together. We shared intimate things about our lives, things about ourselves that other people could not nor would not know, including past relationships. And so she knew about Carolyn, my college love. But yet she loved me, and in my own way, I loved her. She helped me with my doctoral dissertation by assisting with the collation of data. When we left the hospital for the day, she would cook great meals for me, and we simply had a great year together. However.

Since I was going to be initially stationed at the Pearl Harbor Mental Health Clinic, I was going to take my car to Hawaii, and then either leave it there until I returned from the Repose, or sell it. The Navy would ship it from San Francisco to Hawaii. My personal things I had at Bethesda, would be packed and shipped. I had the option of having my things stored, but decided to have my creature comforts sent to my duty station in Hawaii. I didn't have much, but I did have some "stuff," like a rocking chair with a Marquette logo. My mother ordered it for me and had it delivered to me at Bethesda when I started my internship. I loved it, and it was another reminder of Marquette, and how happy I was there too.

I left Bethesda, and Cheryl along with it. It was a bittersweet experience. I was leaving a comfort zone that I had not had since college. I was also excited about the future, and quite frankly the unknown. But also, like when I left Marquette, having packed my car and driving off, I knew that it was something I had to do and wanted to do, but in this case, also ordered to do. My orders read that I had almost two weeks to get to the West Coast, where I would deliver my car for shipment to Hawaii, and catch my flight over. I took this opportunity to drive across the United States. It was going to be great. I would have plenty of needed time by myself, and for myself. After driving through Maryland, Pennsylvania, Ohio and my home in Indiana, I stopped in Milwaukee, of course, and visited the university and some of the old haunts, especially the ones that meant so much to me then and especially later. I even made a point of driving by Norge Village. The memory of my first encounter with Carolyn, came flooding back. I even drove by her old dorm. More than a couple of tears came out of my eyes. I then spent the night at the Pfister Hotel, where Carolyn and I would celebrate a special occasion, like a snow day cancellation of classes, and of course our "pinning." I didn't sleep much that night. The memories, the sweet memories were so vivid.

I left Milwaukee the next morning. And, after driving through Wisconsin and Minnesota, I purposely drove across southern South Dakota, and stopped in Rapid City, to see Mount Rushmore. Well, not only to see Mount Rushmore. I called the old telephone number I had for Carolyn's home, but was told by her brother that she was no longer there, and that she had "married some Indian." Well, so much for that. So, I tucked her pictures back in my duffel bag and continued West.

This country is certainly beautiful. Traveling through Wisconsin and Minnesota, then South Dakota, Colorado, Wyoming, New

Mexico, Arizona, Nevada and California, I didn't find one place I did not like. I did try to stay at military bases when they had Bachelor Officers Quarters or BOQ's, on my journey. For the most part they were modern and fairly Holiday Inn-ish, but, they were comfortable and more importantly, cheap.

I finally arrived at Travis Air Force Base, near San Francisco, and after I checked in my car for shipment, I registered for my flight to Hawaii. Since my flight wouldn't be for another 36 hours, I thought I would check out the city of San Francisco. I was unknowingly smart enough to wear civilian clothes, which I would later find to be one of the best decisions I could ever make from a personal safety, and preservation point of view. I came to learn that the natives there were just not all that friendly to military people, especially those in uniform. I found, however, San Francisco to be a truly beautiful city. I rode a cable car, had lunch at Fisherman's Wharf, and then to the Top of the Mark, for a beer. What a view. What a city.

My flight the next day was uneventful. It was actually a commercial flight contracted with World Airways. Flight attendants, meals, and drinks, it was a great flight. After passing over the Golden Gate Bridge, it was not quite five hours from the West Coast to Honolulu International Airport. And, what a thrill to bank over Diamond Head, on Oahu. Seeing Diamond Head from that vista, for the first time is something I will never forget. I was able to see the Royal Hawaiian, the "Pink Palace," where present day movie stars stayed, and the Aloha Tower, where the movie stars of old would board the Lurline, the luxury ship that would shuttle them back and forth from Hollywood, to the Paradise of the Pacific.

And, then, after the three months temporary duty, or "TDY," at the Mental Health Clinic, at the Naval Station Dispensary, Pearl Harbor, I was on another plane, but this time out of Hickam Air Force Base, which was actually adjacent to Honolulu International Airport. I found myself looking down at the same site I saw three months earlier,

Diamond Head, the Royal Hawaiian, and all of Waikiki Beach, and I was heading away. But, this time, although I was again heading west, now I was really heading West. I was heading to Southeast Asia. I was headed to war. Well, I was not actually headed to war, or so I hoped. I was headed to AH-16, the Repose, which was the Navy hospital ship in the South China Sea. First I would land in Da Nang, in the Republic of Viet Nam. Viet Nam, the Pearl of the Orient. From there I would be helicoptered to the Repose. I was thinking, well, at least I wouldn't have to stay "in country," and would hopefully be safe. God, I didn't want to be here. I wanted to be back at "Mother Bethesda." I wanted to be back at Pearl Harbor. I wanted to be back at Marquette, in Milwaukee, where I didn't care how cold it might be. My mind flashed back to Carolyn, and the day I met her on the way to Norge Village. How could I turn back time? I guess most people wish that at one time or another. I landed in Da Nang, but was on the ground only an hour, just off the tarmac, when a Navy corpsman, dressed in Marine fatigues approached me and reading my name tag greeted me not by my military rank, but by a name I had not heard in several months. "Welcome to Da Nang, Bac Si." I hadn't been called that since Quynh called me that back at Bethesda. It sounded good, but then a bit scary. I was in the land where that was really the language, and that it was where doctors were actually called that. The corpsman's name was Reynolds, and I couldn't tell his rank because of his fatigues, and I wasn't used to seeing a corpsman wearing Marine fatigues. I asked him what his first name was, since I never got used to calling people, including enlisted men, only by their last name.

He shook my hand and said, "Paul, but Bac Si you had better get used to calling me Reynolds. The old man is a stickler for military protocol." So, Reynolds it was, or at least I would try, even though I was not happy with that convention.

"Bac Si, I will be taking you out of here and to the Repose. We are going to catch a Huey out here in about an hour. Do you want me to get you something cold to drink? The local beer here is called "33." Not quite the camel piss I have gotten used to in the past, but there will be Budweiser in the officer's mess on the Repose, but actually the "Ba Ma Ba," isn't too bad. Wanna try it Doc?"

"Sure Paul, why not? You can join me, can't you, or is that verboten too?" I forgot and called him by his first name, instead of Reynolds.

"Affirmative Bac Si, wait here, and I'll get us a couple. Want something to eat? We aren't too close to a pound, so you can eat the food."

"Nah, just a cold one Paul."

I soon learned that Ba Ma Ba, and properly Ma Moui Ba was Vietnamese for Thirty Three. It was a Da Nang brewed beer, initially brewed by the French, who were in Viet Nam before we tried our luck. So, off he went to get us a couple of brewskis. And I had another flashback to my college days in Milwaukee, but this time not about that special coed, but rather thinking about the smell of hops from the Schlitz brewery. Although I was still on the tarmac, I was already getting scared.

"Here you go, Bac Si. I got you some potato chips too. You must be hungry after that flight from Pearl. Did you stop in Pago Pago? That's where we stopped when I came over. Hell of a long flight, isn't it? The helicopter ride out to the Repose from here won't take too long. Less than an hour. You might try to get some shuteye on the way out there, but actually I doubt if that will really happen. Charlie has been more active within the last week. But we haven't had a chopper going out to the Repose hit in over two months. I think they know that we have taken some of the locals who might be friendly to them out for treatment, so they have probably been leaving us alone, and hopefully will.....at least for a while."

Paul Reynolds, the young corpsman, couldn't have been more than 20 years old, not that much younger than me, but he really looked young. I learned later that he was actually my age, and that this was his second tour "in country." He went to the head, while I was drinking my "33." The beer wasn't all that bad, and of course I was a connoisseur of beer, having gone to school in Milwaukee. The chips weren't bad either, but I really was hungry. I didn't realize how hungry I was, and then I remembered that I had not eaten much since I left Hawaii. I guess I was too nervous. Too excited. Was I really going to war? I looked around for someplace I could buy some postcards. Stupid, I thought. We were in a war zone and I was looking for postcards. Unbelievable! Sometimes I amaze myself.

Chapter 8

Over the South China Sea

It was time to get on the helicopter, a Huey. It was not at all what I expected. Oh sure, I had seen these helicopters before, but at a distance. Now I was getting on one. There weren't any steps to help me get on. I had to hop up, and try to get my ass down and swing my legs over. Actually I did quite well, in spite of both Paul and the equally as young looking pilot smiling....no, laughing at my boarding the craft. I found a seat, if you can call it that. Actually it was a box of medical equipment. No seat belt either.

A voice from the front of the craft said, "Hang on Bac Si. We are going to bank pretty steep out of here, and swing hard to the east. The gooks are off to the west, and we want to avoid them, especially since we don't have a gunner on this craft, but not to worry. I have done this a hundred times, and I can do it in my sleep. As a matter of fact, I do do it in my sleep."

The pilot was actually a Marine, but I couldn't tell his rate or rank, also because of his fatigues. Thank God I didn't wear my Navy Blues. I would have looked like such a dork. I was wearing my Khaki's, but I was still wearing a tie. Unbelievable! But, as I found out later, wearing my tie was probably a good thing, when I met the skipper. He turned out to be "old school," and actually expected the docs reporting to his command be Naval Officers first, and health care professionals second. Little did he know that "Hawkeye Pierce" was reporting for duty.

I think he would have dropped a load if he knew I was wearing love beads, although I think that it is often expected that "shrinks" are a little weird, or at least eccentric….and liberal.

But, my focus quickly changed when I heard gunfire, as we were ten minutes out of Da Nang. Paul, had made this trip many times, and told me in no uncertain terms, that those were unfriendlies, and that in spite of any Red Cross identification on the helicopter, we were the target….we were the enemy. Then he said something that scared the hell out of me. "I guess the lull of the past couple of months is over Bac Si. Charlie is after us. We must have pissed them off. Hang tight man, we are going higher. Those are rifle shots you hear, and not rockets, so if we get high enough we are not as good a target, and maybe they'll try to save their ammunition for someone closer."

Sweatingly I thought, "I am in the fucking war! People are trying to kill me. And this isn't even Gary, Indiana, anymore!"

CHAPTER 9

Captain Chuck Caldwell, USMC

Rising above the green landscape of Viet Nam would have been a treat if there weren't people shooting at us. I managed to hold onto the box of medical supplies I was sitting on while I pulled the Nikon out of my duffle bag. I had to take a picture of this. The rice paddies were orderly, and tan, with the green of the jungle surrounding them, and the blue brown mountains behind the jungle. I wondered if there were tigers down there. Certainly there were water buffalo, and Vietnamese bending over picking the rice, wearing their non la's, protecting them from the oppressive heat of the sun. Then I wondered about all the stories I heard about the likelihood that those same Vietnamese farmers were actually Viet Cong, or at least Viet Cong sympathizers. Were they reaching for a rifle or rocket launcher while we thought they were bending down to pick the rice? At any rate, I had to take a picture of this. As if I was on some vacation. Again, sometimes I simply amaze myself. I did take a roll of pictures before we hit the coast, and headed out to sea. Not one of those farmers took aim at us, but from the jungle we did see the tracers of shots being fired at us, and there was no doubt in my mind that it was from Charlie. Captain Chuck Caldwell, our Marine pilot, assured me that it probably was not Viet Cong, but in fact some of the local farmers who truly were sympathetic to the North Vietnamese, either because of ideology or fear, or maybe they were just hedging their bets, betting for and against both sides. Didn't they know that we were here to liberate them from the evils of communism? And if they weren't Viet Cong, then how would you describe them. I soon learned that "they" were the enemy, and that even the friendlies were probably the enemy, at least in some ways.

Heading out over the South China Sea was an experience I would never forget. Leaving the green lushness of Viet Nam, and then seeing nothing but the beautiful blueness of the sea, it almost lulled me into a security of peace. Actually it did. There were no waves, and barely a whitecap. I had heard that some of the troops at an in-country R&R at China Beach, near Da Nang, were actually surfing waves there. How could that be? The sea was so peaceful and calm. I was used to the surf on the North Shore of Oahu. Makaha, the Banzai Pipeline, and even Haleiwa, those were surf spots with great waves. Even Waikiki had great surfing. Surfing in Viet Nam? Impossible! But as we flew away from the coast, my attention shifted back to where I was, and where I was headed.

"Hey Captain, how long to we get to the Repose?"

"Not long, Doc. Maybe another 45 minutes. We are making pretty good time. The skipper isn't expecting us for about another hour and a half. Do you want to make another pass at the coast so you can take some more pictures for the folks back home?"

Under my breath I mumbled, "What a passive-aggressive asshole."

"No, Captain, I got enough. Thanks for your concern though." I wonder what this guy's story is? Here he is, a Marine Captain, and he is ferrying supplies and personnel back and forth from a ship, albeit a hospital ship, to an in-country base, and back. I wonder if that is what he learned at whatever college he attended or if that is what he learned in the Marine Corps. He had to have gone to college if he was an officer. Probably some extension college with an ROTC program. How wrong I was, I later learned.

"Where did you go to school Captain?" I asked. He didn't answer.

I wasn't sure if he ignoring me or if he didn't hear me from the helicopter noise. But we were wearing headphones, so certainly we could hear each other. So, I asked again, but this time I took a different tact. "Hey Captain, did you play college football?"

"As a matter of fact I did."

"You have a southern accent. Did you play for an SEC school?"

"Nope."

Whoa, this guy really is passive-aggressive. I wonder what I did or said to piss him off. It couldn't have been anything I said. I hadn't said much to him. Maybe it was the pictures. But how could taking pictures bother him?

"Did you go through ROTC? How do you like the Corps?" Silence. Hey, I don't need this. Not only don't I want to be here, I don't need to put up with psychopathology from someone who isn't even my patient. I looked at Paul, who was clearly enjoying this and mouthed "what?" He just mouthed back "Let it go Doc. It isn't you. He just lost some buddies in the bush a week ago." The remainder of the flight was calm and quiet, relatively speaking. The rotor whirring of the helicopter was the only sound I heard for the next forty-five minutes.

CHAPTER 10

The Repose

After flying over the surprisingly calm South China Sea for approximately forty-five minutes, I finally heard words. In my headphones I heard Captain Caldwell alerting the Repose that we were approaching, and that we were three minute out. We had made good time.

I heard him say, "AH-16, this is Doc Transport One. We are three clicks out. Requesting permission to land. Requesting landing instructions."

"Roger, Doc Transport, you are cleared to land. Use the aft helipad. We are waiting for you. Were you able to acquire the med box?"

"Affirmative AH-16."

"What about the shrink, Doc Transport?"

"Affirmative AH-16. He is sitting on the med box. See you in about two minutes."

Seeing the gleaming white ship floating in the azure sea was a sight to behold. It appeared so small when I first caught sight of her, five minutes earlier. As we approached her, I saw how big of a ship she was. I don't know why I was surprised. After all, I knew she was a floating hospital, not merely a clinic, and a large hospital at that.

I thought to myself, "there she was, The Angel of the Orient, the Repose, AH-16." She was called the Angel of the Orient because she spent virtually her entire life-saving mission, in Asia, and mostly

Southeast Asia. She served in Korea, and was now saving lives off the coast of Viet Nam. Interestingly both of these wars were not technically called wars, but rather, "conflicts." Tell that to the soldiers, sailors, marines and airmen this floating hospital helped mend or save. She was 665 feet of brilliant white, with a huge red cross painted on her. She was beautiful. As I later learned on my indoctrination tour aboard, she had a displacement of eleven thousand one hundred and forty tons when empty, with fifteen thousand tons maximum. Her beam was seventy-one feet six inches, and had a draft of twenty-four feet. With propulsion of a geared turbine, single screw, her maximum speed was seventeen and a half knots. With no armaments, with the exception of what the Marine guards carried, her personnel capacity was ninety-five officers and six hundred and six enlisted. All of these personnel were there to serve and care for an average daily census of eight hundred patients.

Captain Caldwell was clearly an experienced helicopter pilot. He touched down on the aft deck of the Repose so lightly that I didn't even feel a bump. I did hear the constant roar of the rotor blades, even with the headphones on. Paul, the corpsman signaled me to keep the headphones on. And I am glad that I dutifully obeyed. I actually felt the roar and vibration, albeit slight, of the propeller of the Repose. I would have thought that she was stationery, but she was moving ever so slightly, as she was moving up the coast. I later learned that there was some heavy fighting up north, closer to the DMZ, the Demilitarized Zone, whatever demilitarized zone meant in this war. Since 1954, this was a no man's land at the seventeen parallel, and essentially served as a buffer area between North and South Viet Nam. It was just south of the DMZ where names such as Khe Sahn and Hamburger Hill were becoming known. Reportedly there had just been a significant firefight with a large number of casualties, and the Repose needed to get closer to them, therefore saving much needed time to get the wounded to her. Response time in getting patients to the hospital ship was exactly like the need to get to a hospital on land. Minutes counted.

Paul hopped off the helicopter first. I knew that Captain Caldwell would be the last to get off, as pilots and ship captains always do. I saw him going through his shut down procedure as Paul offered me his hand to help me get off the chopper. I didn't take it. I could get off myself. I wasn't that old, although I was beginning to feel old, seeing all the young faces coming to secure the helicopter. Paul reached for the med box, but I waved him off and told him that I would carry it, forgetting that I still had my duffle bag on board, with all my worldly possessions, at least all my worldly possessions out here in Westpac, the Western Pacific. He sensed that and told me just to get my duffle bag and that he really would, and quite frankly should, get the med box. I was thinking that I just didn't want to give Captain Caldwell, the passive-aggressive, the satisfaction, but Paul was right. I did need to just take care of my own store, my own stuff, my own duffle bag. There would be plenty of time, as I later learned, that I would be carrying other stuff.

The med box did not seem heavy, in Paul's hands. Actually my duffle bag seemed heavier in mine, but that might have been because I was so tired. I really had not slept or rested since I left Pearl Harbor. I sure could use some rack time in my nice, comfortable BOQ room bed. Actually I could just plain use some rack time. I wondered what the accommodations were like on a ship. My guess was that at least on the hospital ships, medical personnel would have at least a modicum of comfort. After all they needed to be well rested so they could devote all their energy to saving lives. But, sleep, I learned, would come later, much later. For now, I just needed to get my bag and get away from the helicopter.

So, I followed Paul, and he reminded me, "Bac Si, remember to call me Reynolds, not Paul. As I told you, the old man is a stickler for protocol."

"Sure thing Paul," I said, grinning at him.

He frowned, but then smiled, then frowned again, as another officer approached us, and said "Lieutenant Staffieri? I am Lieutenant Commander Rosen. You are attached to my unit. Mental Health. I am the chief psychiatrist. Actually I am the only psychiatrist, and you are sorely needed. Your triage and language skills have been expected."

I really didn't know what he meant by that. Maybe he meant triage ability. But, why would language skills be an issue. It started to dawn on me that since we were off the coast of Viet Nam, that my studying Vietnamese might be useful, but why? Were we actually taking on Vietnamese civilians as patients? Actually I did hear that in some emergency cases, a local civilian might be brought to the Repose for emergent care, especially if it was a very interesting case. There would always be emergencies that could warrant the medical skills and facilities aboard a state of the art floating hospital, but the Repose had to care for "our own." That was its stated mission. Our own deserved the best medical care our country could offer. After all, our wounded were serving our country, and that was the least our country could do for them.

CHAPTER 11

Aft Deck on the Repose

Lieutenant Commander Joel Rosen seemed like a pleasant enough guy.

He took my duffle from me saying, "Here, let me take that. I know you have been flying for a day, and that it felt like a week. I know, because that is how I felt."

Walking across the aft deck of the Respose, I was in awe. This floating hospital really was exactly that, a floating major hospital. As a matter of fact, most community hospitals back in the world were not this big. And, with eight hundred patients treated each day, I doubt if many major city hospitals were this big.

I dutifully followed Dr. Rosen across the deck to the lift, which was actually an elevator. We took the elevator up one level, and exited into a passageway. The passageway was actually much larger than I had expected. I guess I thought of the ships I saw on television, where people had to just squeeze by. But then, those might have been submarines. Again, I was in awe at the apparent enormity of this ship. We passed the galley, which led into a mammoth dining area. It reminded me of a college dining hall. There were a couple of people in scrubs, having a cup of coffee. No doubt they were surgeons, since they were still wearing their surgical head covers and had their masks hanging around their necks. They were both looking down at their cups, as if in thought. My thought was, maybe they were depressed. Typical Shrink. Dr. Rosen called out to them, and they looked up.

"This is Dr. Staffieri. He just came aboard. He just joined our band of merry men. He is a psychologist, the bilingual one."

They both nodded, and then looked back down. I thought it was strange why Dr. Rosen had to introduce me as "the bilingual one." I would have thought a simple introduction as another psychologist or psychiatrist would have sufficed. But, I let it pass without pursuing it.

"Before I introduce you to the old man, I'll show you your quarters. Although you will be bunking with me, well not really with me. Our stateroom, so to speak, is shared, divided in half, with a wall separating your quarters from mine. So, sort of think of it as two rooms, with a single door. The officer's shower and head is just down the passageway. Not too close, but close enough." As we entered the room that I was going to share with my new found colleague. I was pleasantly surprised. It looked like I was also going to have my own desk. Actually, I thought, my BOQ room back at Bethesda, wasn't this nice. And, at Bethesda, the head and showers were way down the hall, and clearly very communal, much like a college dorm.

Dr. Rosen placed my duffle on my rack, my bed, and said, "Do you want a couple of minutes to wash up before I take you up to the Captain, or do you want to get it over with now?"

I said, "Hey, let's go." So, off we went, down the passageway, back to the elevator, and once inside Rosen pushed the button marked "upper deck." Upper Deck, humm, I thought, just like in Comiskey Park, the home of the Chicago White Sox. But that was another time, in another incarnation for me. We stepped off and out of the elevator, facing a relatively short passageway. At the far end of the passageway I saw a wooden door, with a wooden doorframe, unlike the doors I noticed throughout the ship. The door was highly polished, and had a sign attached to it, with the Captain's name on it. It read CAPT Hewlet L. Baker, MC, USN. I was about to meet my commanding officer. Little did I know then that he would be so life affecting for me. But, I fairly quickly found out.

CHAPTER 12

The Commanding Officer

Joel Rosen knocked on the polished wood door, and from inside the room I heard, "Enter."

Joel opened the door and led the way in, and greeted the captain by his first name, which surprised me. I thought he said that the old man, as he referred to him, was a stickler for protocol.

Then he said, "Captain, Lieutenant Thomas Staffieri here, just came aboard, and is reporting in. I have already shown him his quarters, and we stowed his duffle and came directly here."

"Very good Joel, thanks."

The Captain extended his hand and said, "Lieutenant Staffieri, Dr. Staffieri, I am Captain Baker. I am the commanding officer of the Hospital Ship Repose, but you probably already surmised that. My guess is that you have already been apprised that I am somewhat a stickler for protocol, military protocol. That is probably true, but the reality is that it is only whenever it is necessary from a military point of view. First and foremost I am a doctor, and as such, the care for my charges is my primary concern, and that includes the medical personnel as well as our patients. Oh yes, I know that the responsibility for the ship is my legal and military obligation, but let me be clear, curing and healing our patients is my mission. And, I expect that is what all the health care professionals under my command are here for, and is what they are all about. At least that is what I hope, but more importantly, what I expect and demand."

With this introduction, I knew that I liked this guy, and could respect him, even in my somewhat rebellious way. I knew he must have noticed my love beads tangled in my dog tags. Maybe he was giving me a pass on my hippiness, on my first few minutes aboard. But maybe not, since I noticed a picture on his desk of a couple of young girls, his daughters no doubt, wearing tie dyed shirts and bandanas. Maybe he was simpatico to the counter culture. I doubt if he was simpatico to any anti-war movement, but maybe at least to the "hippie" uniform du jour.

"Pleasure to meet you sir. I do share your commitment to the care and welfare of our patients. I am looking forward to my assignment here, although quite frankly I am a little curious about how I, as a psychologist, am going to fit into the psychological treatment team. I know that you have Doctor, I mean Lieutenant Commander Rosen here, but I am a little curious about why I was asked for. Why me?"

The Captain merely smiled and said, "We'll talk later, once you get situated. Perhaps you will join me in my quarters for dinner at 1800. We can discuss your role here and there, then."

I wondered what he meant by "here and there," but replied "Yes, sir, I look will look forward to it. Thank you sir."

At that point he said to both of us, "That will be all."

We both said, "Aye, aye sir," in unison, and made an about face and left the Captain's office.

Leaving Captain Baker's office I felt a bit relieved. I didn't know if I could hack rigid military protocol. Certainly I saw a bit of it back at Mother Bethesda, and much more back at Pearl Harbor, but I was pretty much insulated from it because of being in the Medical Service Corps. Maybe it was because it really was not expected that docs, or even nurses for that matter, saw themselves as first Naval officers and then health care professions. It was probably assumed by most of the Black Shoe Navy, which meant Line Officers, that docs, of whatever ilk, would not stay in the military for a career, or even actually know what to do in a real military situation. I did have to admit, however, that I did like being a Naval Officer, and not just because of the uniforms. I did like, even with my rebellious streak, the structure of the military. Maybe it was because of a basic behavioral principal that said, in effect, that all schizophrenics and all normals, and all of us in between, respond to one thing, structure and firm limit setting. Without structure or definite limits, the world would have chaos. The examples frequently used to make this behavioral point was, that if there were no traffic laws, or if each taxpayer decided to pay their taxes on different days or months.....Chaos.

Joel and I didn't say much on the way back to our shared quarters. And, I was surprised that I was able to pretty much find the right passageways back to the quarters, without directions from Joel. Actually though, I have always had a fairly good sense of direction. We came to our quarters, and I was really looking forward to lying down on my rack and closing my eyes for a bit. Closing my eyes would have to be, in fact, for just a bit, since I would have to take a shower and get into a clean uniform before I had to meet with Captain Baker, at 1800. It dawned on me that I had not had a shower in going on 48 hours, and that I must really be "ripe."

I thanked Joel for the introduction, and also for meeting me at the chopper and helping to get me settled in. I told him that I was going to rest a bit, take a shower and then get up to have my introduction dinner with the Captain. I assumed that the Captain met with, and had an introductory dinner with all the officers reporting to duty on his ship. I stretched out on my bunk and reached over and unzipped my duffle bag. I took out my personal folder. In it I had my orders, which I inadvertently had neglected to present to the Captain, and my personal pictures, including the ones of the Marquette coed of years ago. I really don't know why I was keeping those particular pictures of Carolyn so close, but they were on the top of the stack of pictures that I brought with me. My family pictures were framed, but the ones of Carolyn weren't. I recall putting them into my folder and bag at the last minute. I am not sure I know why I did that. I had been moving them from desk drawer to desk drawer during graduate school and internship. I had not been dwelling on them, or her, over the years, but rather just when things got a little tough for me at times, or generally when I heard something about Marquette, but not always. Marquette always had a good basketball team, especially after they dropped football following the 1960 season. But, since Marquette frequently made the NCAA tournament, or at least the NIT, generally I might have a flashback to that very warm memory. But, having been told by her brother, when I stopped in that little town in South Dakota, that she had "married some Indian," I tried to keep that warm memory in abeyance. Sometimes it worked and sometimes it didn't. But, life goes on. So, I put Carolyn's pictures back in my folder, and took out my orders and placed them on the desk next to my bunk. I placed a picture of my family, small as it might be, next to the orders packet, set the alarm on my runners watch for 1715, and closed my eyes.

My eyes opened at 1710, after an hour nap. My internal alarm, which I have had all my life, always alerts me to when I need to awaken. It also helps that I am a very light sleeper. Always have been. And, I also sleep hot. I need very few covers, and although snuggling under a comforter, either back in Milwaukee or Bethesda, sounds delicious, I usually couldn't wait to move the covers off of me and over to "her" side of the bed.

The medical staff quarters were actually pretty quiet, although I soon learned that when the ship was underway, the screw, or propeller, made a rhythmic drone. And, for a light sleeper, that would probably keep me from getting much sleep at all. Things on this day, however, were quiet. I took my Dopp kit down to the head and shaved and showered. I felt like a new man. I put on my dress khakis, complete with a tie, and looked in the mirror and combed my hair. My eyes looked a bit baggy, but not puffy, and they were not bloodshot as one would expect after a day flight, jet lag, and minimal sleep. The Captain already saw me, and he knew that I had been traveling for the last twenty-four hours, so he had to know and appreciate how tired I was. But, looking in the mirror, the face looking back at me said tired and was beginning to show some miles, or at least years.

I closed the door to my side of the quarters, more out of habit than because of security. After all, what did I have that anyone would want or could steal, and besides, we were all Naval Officers and doctors of various types.

Walking past the galley and mess hall, the smell of onions being fried hit my olfactory. It smelled good, but actually I would prefer the smell of garlic frying in some olive oil, like my mother do, before she would sauté' some spinach. But, the smell, and the olfactory flashback, quickly disappeared as I approached the elevator that would take me up to the Captain's office. Maybe what was being cooked and prepared was going to be for what I assumed was going to be my welcome aboard dinner with the Captain. The lift again took me directly to the short passageway to the Captain's office. I knocked on the polished wooden door, and waited a moment. When the Captain had not answered after a minute, I knocked again. I heard the Captain's voice again, but this time it sounded a bit more gruff.

"Enter Lieutenant Staffieri."

I let myself in and stood at attention, as best I knew how, since Medical Service Corps officers were typically not afforded the opportunity to learn the correct way to stand at attention, salute, and in general, know the standards which senior officers might expect.

But, I must have passed muster because the Captain said, "Relax Tom, no real formality this evening. I am glad you could join me for dinner."

As if I really had a choice about having dinner in the Captain's office my first night aboard.

"We will discuss your duties and mission here and in-country, while we have dinner."

What did he mean by "my mission here and in-country?" In-country meant actually going into Viet Nam, and that was where the war is. No one said anything to me about going "in-country." I was there to deal with mental health issues, and make some decisions about whether someone was psychotic or not, or whether someone was faking just to get out of the Marine Corps or the war zone. I was happy doing psychological evaluations and treatment back on Oahu, and certainly back at Bethesda. I thought back to what my friend George Chase said to me, back at the Bethesda Naval Hospital, when I received my orders, "You're going to friggin' war."

At first I didn't notice him, but standing by the bookcase near the bulkhead at the left side of the door to the office, partially obstructed by the door when it opened, was Marine Captain Chuck Caldwell. He smiled a toothy grin and extended his hand to me, and not in what I would have expected to be his passive-aggressive manner.

"Lieutenant Staffieri, may I call you Tom, I am Chuck. Sorry that we appeared to get off on the wrong foot. Sometimes my social graces leave much to be desired. I tend to shut down, and come across as a real ass-hole some times. Please forgive me if I came across that way with you on the chopper ride out here."

I shook his hand and told him that there were no hard feelings, and that I certainly understood having a long day, and having to ferry around some Navy Shrink, and on top of that getting shot at. I looked at Captain Baker with a quizzical look. He clearly understood my confusion.

"I know you must be wondering why I included Captain Caldwell to what you probably thought was a 'welcome aboard.' It really is a welcome aboard, Tom, but also a chance to discuss some nuances of why you are here, and why now. I think we should probably have a bite to eat first, and I do have a bottle of Pinch Scotch that might take the edge off your apprehension and the residuals of your long days journey here. Do you drink Scotch? Do you know Pinch? Of course you do, it is in your folder. You don't drink much, but when you do, your drink of choice is scotch, and you prefer Pinch, is that not right?"

"Yes sir, but I am a little surprised that my scotch preference would be in my personnel folder. And yes sir, I would love a bit of Pinch, on the rocks, if you don't mind. It really has been a long day."

I couldn't remember the last time I had a scotch. I think it may have been at The Palm, my favorite restaurant in D.C., a couple of nights before I checked out of Bethesda. The Neuropsychology staff had a little going away party for me, and they knew that The Washington Palm was my favorite restaurant. In addition to the gargantuan portions of food, they don't skimp on their drinks, and besides that, I was a friend of the maitre d', and he always made sure I had the best "high vis" table, especially when I had a date. Those tables were usually reserved for the high rolling lobbyists, members of Congress, or other Washington personage. But knowing the maitre d' was a definite asset. I really did like living in the D.C. area.

Captain Baker offered a toast. "To our Country, our Navy, and our Mission."

Both Captain Caldwell and I said "here, here," at the same time.

The Captain sat first, at a table set up in his office. Captain Caldwell and I each sat on opposite sides of the table, flanking his left and right. The food had already been placed in serving dishes, prime rib, mashed potatoes, creamed spinach, and bread and butter. Again, much like The Palm.

I spoke first. "Captain, you said something earlier that, quite frankly, threw me for a loop. You referred to my mission here and in country. Am I to assume that I will actually be going in country, and not merely to catch a flight back to Hawaii or CONUS?" CONUS was military jargon for Continental United States.

Captain Baker and Captain Caldwell both looked at each other, and both of their moods appeared to change from congenial to serious. I thought, oh oh here it comes. We began to eat without either the Captain or Caldwell saying too much. Obviously they were avoiding going into anything, at least until I was, no doubt, fattened up for the kill. They talked about the Repose, its mission, its successes, and some of its failures, but for the most part, the conversation was merely informative, and largely benign. Then came the offer of a cigar, which I declined.

"Did anyone either at Bethesda or at Pearl mention to you what your assignment out her in Westpac might be, Tom? I mean certainly you must have had some inkling of why you might be assigned to a couple of, shall we say, more temporary duties? As you may know, more senior psychologists were passed up for a Hawaii assignment, as well as duty on the Repose, especially if they were temporary assignments. And typically, psychiatrists are assigned here, rather than psychologists, since medication, at least in the short term, is used in general triage or emergency situations."

I did not reply immediately, and let it sink in before I responded.

"Yes sir, I did wonder a bit about that, and I guess quite frankly, I thought that my language skills might be a variable, but also since I did the screenings for isolated duties at McMurdo, in the Antarctic, that that might be something for which I was considered. Not the Antarctic, but maybe assessing men under stress, and their reactions, well, maybe that was something that might be important in a war theatre."

Captain Baker smiled and replied, "Very astute Tom, and right on target. Language skills and stress reactions, you clearly have skills in both, and the Navy knew that almost as soon as your internship at Bethesda began. You apparently even gave talks on stress reaction to isolation, and the motivational advantage of stress. Can you tell me how your interest in that came about Tom? Also, I would like to know about your language fluency, primarily in French and Vietnamese."

"Yes sir," I replied. I think I can date the beginning of my interest in stress reaction to when I read Joost Merloo's "The Rape of the Mind." Our reaction to stress is really pretty interesting, both the negative reaction, which most people associate with stress, as well as any positive reaction, which we might call the advantages of stress. I wrote my doctoral dissertation on stress reactions in children. Insofar as my language fluency is concerned, I have always had a knack for languages. Perhaps it was because back in Gary, Indiana, where I grew up, if you couldn't conduct business in a bunch of languages you would be lost." I grew up speaking Italian, which was essentially my first language. I didn't really know much English until I started first grade. We lived in an area where all the Italians lived, and Italian was spoken almost exclusively. Spanish and Portuguese were so close to Italian, that they were fairly easy to master. That, and the fact that the significant Hispanic and Portuguese population, and friends, insisted that I learn those languages, especially if I was expecting to date their sisters or daughters. Latin as an altar boy was also pretty easy for me because of the Italian. But no one really spoke Latin, even the priests. I took French and German in college, and then had to take either French or German as a language requirement for my Master's. I took French. Then, I had to take the other language, German, as the language requirement for the Doctorate. I really didn't like German, so I didn't keep up with it. French was very much like Italian, so it remained fairly easy for me to keep up with. Insofar as Vietnamese is concerned, with the war starting in 1965, or actually before then, with our advisors, I heard more and more about the people, its culture and its language, so I started dabbling in it. When I got to Bethesda, I saw people who were directly affected by the war. Some were returning military. Some were dependants. And clearly they had all been affected by the war. They spoke the language. I liked them, and started learning it, and the rest, as they say, is history."

Chuck Caldwell leaned over and said to me, "Ban co chong lai chien tranh?"

I thought I knew that to mean "are you against the war?" in Vietnamese.

I said "Xin loi. Toi khong hieu." (I am sorry. I don't understand.)

He repeated "Ban co chong lai chien tranh?"

Then I immediately responded "Da. Toi hieu." (Yes, I understand.) "Khong." (No). I meant that I was not against the war.

He responded in English, "Good."

I guess he saw my love beads when we were on the chopper and made an assumption about where I stood on whether the United States should be in Viet Nam. Maybe that is why he seemed to shut down after we were airborne, on our flight out to the Repose. But I wondered first, why he would ask me that, and second, how did this marine helicopter pilot know so much Vietnamese.

He nodded at Captain Baker and said, "His Vietnamese is pretty good, sir. As a matter of fact his accent is from up near the north, probably Hue City."

Captain Baker said "Good, now let's get down to business, shall we?"

The old man seemed like a pretty good guy. He didn't beat around the bush, nor did he try to sugar coat things or blow smoke up my ass. That had been tried by the best of them. I really did know my business, and I could spot a phony easier than most. My psychology and psychiatry colleagues generally have a tendency to feel that they should believe virtually everything a patient says to them, within reason of course, but typically to not pass judgment or apply one's own values or beliefs onto the person in front of them. For the most part I did too, but there was always a little something in the back of my mind that gave me a sort of sixth sense. That saved me from getting hurt back home, be it Gary, or in college, and definitely in the Navy. After all, the Navy was the government, and as the rhetorical question goes, "Can you trust the government?" But, I also knew that "paranoia will destroya," so I did let many things pass without analyzing everything.

The Captain was direct and too the point, and I liked that.

"Tom, your stay on the Repose will be relatively brief, at least for now. I would love to have you on staff for the remainder of your tour, but your skills are needed in country, and will hopefully lessen our patient load, by lessening American casualties. I will keep you aboard for ten days, and then you will be reassigned to the Fleet Marines. You will head out to Da Nang, then Saigon, and then, unfortunately, I expect, up north, close to the DMZ, or maybe even close to the Cambodian border. Although the NVA, the North Vietnamese Army, and the Viet Cong have been fairly predictable, they are definitely planning something. Our intelligence has picked up some rumblings of something big coming. Whether that is next week, next month, we don't know. We are having a hard time cracking their new codes. If we can get to a high-ranking NVA officer, and get any information about what is being planned, we might be able to intercept any assault, and save countless American lives. You might be asked to do things you have never done before, and which you might have some qualms about. Hopefully not, but once you are off this ship you are no longer under my command, control, or protection. I am sorry, son, but we both have orders. Captain Caldwell here will fill in the blanks, as he can. We'll talk again tomorrow. Try to get some rest. Are you sure you don't want to have another scotch before you go?"

"No, sir, thank you. I think I will just try to hit the sack. Good night sir."

"Good night Tom. Captain Caldwell, see that Tom has what he needs. Good night."

We took our leave. After we left the Captain's office area, I turned and asked, "Where did you learn your Vietnamese, Chuck?"

He simply smiled and said, "Tom, why don't you just get some rest now, and I will try to explain everything, or at least everything I know, tomorrow morning, OK?"

I nodded my assent, and we didn't say anything else as we approached my quarters. I entered my quarters, sat on my bed, and put my head in my hands and wondered, what in the hell I had gotten myself into. I looked up, and Joel, my quarter's mate, was just standing there. He just looked at me, and didn't say a word.

After a very long minute of neither of us saying anything, I finally said, "Joel, I don't want to talk about it right now. Can we talk tomorrow?"

He simply said, "Certainly Tom, see you tomorrow. If you need anything, or if you just need to talk before you fall asleep, well you know all you have to do is ask. Good night Tom. Try to get some sleep. You must be exhausted."

Needless to say, I didn't sleep well that night. Again, I have never been a good sleeper, save perhaps when I was in college. Maybe it was because then, I didn't have too any cares of real importance, other than grades, and my preoccupation with the girlfriend du jour, and most intensely, Carolyn. Usually however, one of Milwaukee's greatest products, beer, took the edge off and put me to sleep.

0530 came around quickly. I didn't get much sleep, although I was able to rest. Since I really didn't eat much at the meeting with the Captain and Chuck, I was famished. I changed into my work khakis and headed down to the mess area. There were still not too many there, although to my surprise, Joel was there, and he was having coffee with Chuck. I went through the chow line and said I would like to have some scrambled eggs, bacon, and toast. The coffee urn was at the end of the line, and I poured myself a cup, actually a mug. I learned early on that the reason coffee is generally in a mug aboard ships is a carry over from the old days when sailors standing watch needed to warm their hands, so they kept them wrapped around the mug for warmth. As a Naval Officer, however, in public, and not merely formal occasions, the officer was expected to use a cup and saucer. Well not on this ship. We were all sailors, regardless of rank or rate. So, mugs it was.

I took my tray over to Joel and Chuck and asked if I could join them, or was this a session. We all smiled, and probably all thought about whether it was a psychotherapy session. They both bid me to sit and join them. At first the conversation centered around whether or not I got any sleep, being my first time in a bunk aboard a ship. I confessed that I was a light sleeper anyway, and being on a ship only probably added to my sleep disturbance. But, the unspoken was deafening.

" I was thinking about what my duties here might be, and why I was going to be sent into Viet Nam. Chuck, I know that you know why, and apparently so do you Joel. Can either or both of you fill me in?"

Both of them looked down into their coffee mugs, waiting for the other to start the information briefing. It was getting, I feared, a bit ominous.

"Come on fellas, say something. I can surmise that there might be something covert in my horizon. Level with me. I really thought I was going to be here to do more of a triage duty, but figured there might be something else as well. I am not clueless."

Joel started. "Tom, you are, in fact here to help out with triage. We need to intervene with some of the clearly psychotic patients as well as those who are experiencing incapacitating anxiety reactions to combat. You know enough about psychotropic medications that you can make some of those decisions, and of course I will be here to back you up if there is a true medical issue or medication combination issue. Your training, as I have read, indicates that you are well trained in neuro-psychology, and have probably as much didactic training in brain function, certainly brain behavior, as I do. It is the other part of your training that is, no doubt, what makes you even more valuable. Your language skills. That superimposed on your dissertation dealing with stress reactions and stress as a motivational factor, well you appear to be, as they say, 'da man.'"

Chuck merely smiled and drank his coffee. When he finally spoke he said, "Tom, your Vietnamese is pretty good, especially for never having been in country. How is your French? The reason I ask is that some of these gooks are products of the education from the French nuns who were here, and some of which still are. Sometimes they will feign that they don't understand our Vietnamese, but then smile, nay downright laugh, when we say something to them in French. That is the dead giveaway. Once they smirk, laugh or even smile, we know they understand us, and then we have them. Then we can extract information from them. But, to have someone fluent in both, well, that is not only a plus, but in some cases necessary. And, on top of that, to have someone who knows about motivation, stress, and breaking points, well how sweet it is."

I was in a state of bewilderment, but slowly it all began to come together for me. I really wasn't there just to evaluate and treat patients; I was also there to interrogate them. Who the "them" were was a different matter, but I could only guess. It didn't take a rocket scientist to figure out that there wasn't a big need to speak Vietnamese and/ or French to our own troops. That meant Charlie, Victor Charles, the VC. Now how and when was I going to do that?

"Joel, did you ask for me to come out here? Are you really the only mental health doc on the Repose? Chuck, what are you really doing here? Really, why am I here?"

Chuck spoke up and said, "Hold on, Tom. We'll tell you everything we can. And, actually I know more than Dr. Rosen here, so let him off the hook. He really wanted you here because you really do have a skill with stress that could help some of the combat patients, and actually some of the non-combat patients med-evaced to the Repose, as well. There is a need to know aspect here, so maybe Joel will leave us now?"

Joel nodded and didn't argue. He didn't say anything. He picked up his mug and left the table. Chuck called after him, "Thanks Joel."

"Tom, what I am about to tell you is clearly top secret. I know you are cleared, but I need to know that you are fully aware of the ramifications of top secret. And, perhaps as importantly, as we alluded to when we had dinner with Captain Baker last night, there might be some problems with possible ethical issues of the American Psychological Association. Both the American Psychological Association and the American Psychiatric Association have taken positions on their members' participation in interrogations. And, when some, shall we say questionable techniques to extract vital information from enemy personnel, are used, both groups really dig in their heels. Unfortunately, many of the people developing and putting forward these positions, no matter how lofty they may ideally be, simply do not always mesh with the realities of war. Do you understand, Tom?" Of course I understood. I may be a professional psychologist, and dedicated to the alleviation of human suffering, but I am also a realist. The Jesuits drummed realism into me, as they also did humanism and human dignity." But, I could see that the potential for an ethical dilemma existed for me. I would have to learn more before I could make a decision about what I could do or not do, using my professional skills. I needed Chuck to tell me more, and preferable all, about what I was being asked to do.

"Chuck, I need you to tell me all you can about what I am really doing here and what is next."

He then smiled and said, "Hey Tom, why don't you just know, that for the next week or so, you will be attending to patients aboard the Repose. As you see the guys you are treating, and hear what they have endured and seen, you might have a new appreciation for what you might have to do; things you never thought you would have to do. I will tell you this Tom, you will be expected to directly confront the enemy. You will see Charlie, and you will deal with him first hand."

Well that certainly scared the hell out of me.

CHAPTER 13

Making Rounds

Joel had me paged. I joined him on the Neurology ward on the treatment deck. Actually there were two medical decks. One was a dedicated surgical deck. The operating theatre, or I should say theatres took up an entire deck. At least twenty surgeries cold take place at the same time on the Repose. Clearly the facilities were top notch. Some of the finest surgeons in the Navy were saving lives and limbs on the Repose. No doubt some of these surgeons would go on, when they left the Navy, and head up major surgical programs in some of the best hospitals in the world, including Johns Hopkins, Columbia, The Mayo Clinic, and others. Many of these surgeons were actually straight out of top echelon residency programs, where they were allowed to finish their training, funded by the Navy, and then serve their commitment for three years. If I needed surgery, I thought, I would certainly want these surgeons to operate on me. The medical deck was equally impressive. There were various wards for several of the medical specialties and sub specialties. There was even a section for Infectious Disease, which one generally doesn't associate with anything typically acute. But, given being in Southeast Asia, some of the diseases could, in fact, be acute and not only life threatening but easily communicable, and potentially able to decimate an entire company of soldiers or Marines within days, if not hours.

And then there was the area in which I was most interested; my own. Neuropsychology, or actually Neurology and Psychiatry. With a great many traumatic brain injuries, the assessment and emergent treatment of head wounds was a necessity. The devastation of a brain injury was overwhelming, with a general prognosis being very poor for not only return to duty but effective life functioning back in the States. Many of these patients would, no doubt, end up in a Veteran's Administration Hospital, close to their home of record. The surgeons would typically do a great job in repairing the structural damage done by a bullet to the brain, and the patient's life being saved, but the rehabilitation of the wiring of the brain, and the brain behavior components, well that was a different matter, one within the realm of Neurology and Psychiatry. Contrary to popular belief, Psychology and Psychiatry didn't just focus on whether you loved your mother and hated your father. Those issues might be important, but not here. There were more significant issues at stake here. If our service didn't do it's job, then the soldier patients who "circled the drain," would wish they had gone down the drain, and not live with the devastation of their injury. Psychologically, the trauma of losing a limb, or in some cases limbs, was equally as devastating as a brain injury. It was here that immediate psychological intervention was necessary. The Mobile Army Surgical Hospitals, or MASH, simply did not have the luxury of treating non-physical wounds or injuries. The most acute or serious ones would be flown to the Repose, unless it was determined at the MASH unit that they could last until they made it to a Naval Hospital, in Japan, or some other land facility, including back in CONUS, the acronym for Continental U.S.

Joel walked me through several of the medical units, and introduced me to doctors, nurses, corpsmen, and other medical and administrative staff. This, I thought, was really a comprehensive facility. I expected it to be, but the extent of the facility was impressive. He handed me a chart on a young marine who had shrapnel wounds to the left side of his head. In spite of his wounds he would laugh uncontrollably. The question was, now that he was "repaired," what was the next step. Was there a functional or psychological basis for his laughter? Although his head injury had been severe, the neurosurgeons had really repaired his brain, and the area that controls emotions in general, and laughter, in particular, was, in fact, now intact and at least theoretically as good as new. Was there some secondary gain here? Was this patient now delusional? Again, our mission on the Repose was not to do any actual psychotherapy, but rather to determine and dispose. But, an immediate course of treatment was needed before we could send him off to his next destination, whether it was a hospital in Japan or at home. Either way, this young man was not going back into combat. At Bethesda Naval Hospital, or more formally The National Naval Medical Center, many of these wounded warriors after they were essentially triaged out of the war zone, hospital ship, or hospital in Japan, were received and treated on a longer-term basis. Part of the reason for this, other than for strictly medical necessity reasons, was that it was a residency program facility for a number of specialties, including surgery, neurology, and psychiatry and psychology. Dependants were also treated at Bethesda, and that is where my clinical training was provided. The Navy offered a child psychology program there and that was another reason I jumped at the opportunity to train there, as well as to fulfill the military requirement that most guys were facing, the draft. The draft lottery came later. My age group was still being greeted and selected by "our friends and neighbors," though the draft boards.

I knew, or at least believed, that I would not be seeing any children in evaluation or treatment after my internship at Bethesda. However, as I toured and made rounds with Joel, on the Repose, I became aware that there were, in fact, pediatric patients being treated, both medically as well as in surgery. It appeared that the Navy was also taking care of some of the Vietnamese children. I learned shortly that a number of them, too, had head injuries, but most of them were because of severe Napalm burns. Napalm, that gelatinous oily substance that stuck to skin while burning. The surgeons had to graft skin, where skin was completely burned off, by the Napalm that burned everything in its path. I could only imagine the scars those poor little kids would have as a result of the Napalm, not only the physical scars but the psychological scars as well. I thought back to little Quynh, my little Vietnamese patient at Bethesda. One of these kids could have been her. I asked one of the Navy nurses if anyone was speaking Vietnamese to these kids, the ones undergoing the grafting. A couple of them had their mothers along, but many of them lost their mothers in the furnace of the napalm. And, no matter how necessary the napalming had to be, the effect on these little children was staggering. So, when I was directed to one of the little patients who was alone, a nine-year-old little girl, I had to talk to her in her native language.

"Xin Chao."

She looked up at me and tried to mouth the Vietnamese for hello, back to me. I held her little hand and tried to assure her, the best I could, that she was going to be ok. I wondered if she ever would just be just OK. I thought again, of my little patient, Quynh, back at Bethesda. She would be about the same age as this little girl. There was a friggin' war going on out there. When would all of this fighting and suffering end? What was my mission in all of this? I believed in the cause, and thought our involvement was just, in spite of what some of my fellow classmates and some psychologists thought. If I didn't believe in it I would never have accepted my commission.

Joel caught up with me and wanted me to see some of the rest of the hospital ship. It really was cavernous, but extremely well organized. And, everyone aboard who I met or saw, seemed dedicated. I was anxious to get started on whatever it was I was going to be assigned to do by Joel. Clearly there was not a psych unit aboard, but clearly there was a need for psychological intervention. My guess is that the staff would also be in need of stress management as well as coping strategies as a result of seeing what they have seen. Seeing human suffering, and especially in such an intense manner, has to take its toll on the caregivers, so they need an outlet, a catharsis therapy if nothing else. I knew that in some, they would take these issues home with them, only to surface later in life, if they didn't deal with those issues now. And even if they did deal with those demons now, there was no guarantee that they wouldn't be haunted later.

It seemed that everyone knew Joel, and for a shrink he was outgoing and not very "shrinky." That was good because I didn't see myself as particularly "shrinky" either. My orientation was that I would rather talk about what is right with someone rather than focus on what might be wrong with someone. And, as the saying goes, Freud was supposed to have said, "A cigar can just be a good smoke. It doesn't have to be a phallic symbol." Most people called him by his name, and not by his rank, doc, or doctor. Even some of the corpsmen, who were enlisted, called him Joel, unless one of the line officers was around, or one of the senior nurses. The nurses were held in high esteem, as far as I could tell. And, all the Navy nurses I saw so far on board were good looking. I know that helped the morale of wounded patients who were recovering. That certainly was the case back at Bethesda.

"Tom, we are going to go over to the neurology unit. That is where you and I will primarily hang out. What do you think so far?"

Although I had not seen too much of everything, I did have a good feel about the services and the professionalism of the staff. I could see, however, that they were overwhelmed. You can actually see it in their eyes. It was what I would later come to recognize as the thousand yard stare."

I said, "Joel, I am really impressed and can't wait to start seeing patients. You will have to tell me what to do of course, at least until I get acclimated. But have you been in country yet? Have you seen where all of this begins? Since I gather I am not going to be here long, at least at first, I guess long term care or treatment protocols are not on my horizon here?"

He smiled and said, "I was in country once, for a week, but it was just to check on a couple of docs out in a MASH unit. It seems they were drinking so many martinis that they couldn't operate, or I should say wouldn't operate. It turns out that they got so sick on their food and drink, on their R and R, in Bangkok, that they actually became psychotic. It was almost a "folie a deux", two people sharing the same hallucination, or in this case delusion. After we detoxed them, they were fine. Fine and grateful. I was happy to get back aboard ship, however. The sound of gunfire scares the hell out of me. I'm from Kansas. People don't shoot at us in Kansas."

I laughed, since I was from Gary, and everyone shoots at you there.

The day passed quickly. We didn't even have a chance for lunch, although we did grab a snack at one of the nurse's stations. It is amazing how peanuts and coffee can fill you up. At dinnertime I was hungry. Dinnertime aboard a hospital ship is not really a scheduled meal because most medical personnel are on different schedules and more often than not are tending to a patient and cannot just leave because their stomach is growling, or because they are only serving dinner at 1800 to 2000 hours. It just doesn't work that way in medicine, and especially on the Repose. Dinner is pretty much always available throughout the evening, as are the other meals throughout the day. The food was actually pretty good, and the choices were varied. As a psychologist, typically evening work was not an issue. Here however, I was to find out, psychological services are always needed, and it wasn't just the "Go tell it to the Chaplin" problems. If it wasn't assessing or reassuring a patient, it was assessing or reassuring the staff. I would see first hand how related psychology, psychiatry, and neurology, are, and discovered first hand, the newly emerging field of neuropsychology. Psychiatry and Neurology were always closely linked. Even their Boards were the singular Board of Psychiatry and Neurology, albeit with separate focus, depending on the particular specialty, Psychiatry or Neurology. Joel began to be a mentor to me almost immediately, and that mentorship developed into a close friendship, that would last for many years. He asked me if I minded him showing him the ropes on the Repose, on the Neurology unit, as well as instructing me, as much as he could, in battlefield psychiatry. I assured him that I was eager to learn, and that if there was anything, anything at all, that he could teach me or even help me improve, if he saw me doing something wrong, to please teach me. I think he appreciated that. So off we went, and grabbed a stack of charts. My indoctrination began.

Joel left me on my own, after he sat me at one of the nursing stations with a rack of charts in front of me. One of the nurses brought me a cup of coffee while I began reading through some of the charts. One chart in particular struck my attention. Another head trauma of course, but this time the behavioral aspects didn't jive with where the injury was located, and it turned out to be a South Vietnamese official who had been injured in an explosion in a bar in Saigon, one I learned from one of the Marine guards, that was frequented by G.I.'s. I wondered if that was usual, for South Vietnamese officials hanging out with G.I.'s or where they hung out. I decided to go and see this patient. When I greeted the patient in Vietnamese he shook his head, so I switched to French. He still shook his head, so what else was left, English. He acknowledged me in English, but then looked away. Was he distracted by something or was he not processing?

A corpsman came up behind me and said, "Sir, he always does that, so it is not you. We can't figure out what is wrong. Also, we can't figure out how he got here. He must be someone important and was helicoptered out to us. We probably have to send him back to Da Nang, and let his own people try to figure it out."

"Let me have a shot at him today, and I will also discuss it with LCDR Rosen. I am sure we can figure something out."

I re-read his chart, and something just didn't make sense. Why was this probably high-ranking South Vietnamese national with a head injury that he sustained at an explosion at a G.I. bar, now communicating only in English rather than his native tongue. Generally when people have a stroke or other brain injury, and their communication cognition is impaired, they revert to their first or native language. My gut was that he just didn't want to communicate in Vietnamese or French. Soon I learned that I was right.

Once the corpsman left, the patient spoke to me in Vietnamese and said, "Bac Si, I don't want to go back to Saigon. Something bad is going to happen there soon. My brother has told me so."

I tried to pursue this with him but then he simply shut down. I tried for the next fifteen minutes to get him to open up again, but to no avail. I told him that I would be back after I checked on some other patients. Instead, I went to see Joel, and told him what transpired. Joel was a real common sense psychiatrist, which was, as far as I was concerned, unusual in the field. Since something about danger, or something bad being imminent, even if it was either delusional or from someone with a head injury, we both agreed that it was probably better to err on the side of caution, rather than blowing it off or chalking it up to the ramblings of a mad man. So he suggested that we go and see Captain Caldwell. I found that a bit odd. Why not Captain Baker, our commanding officer? We located the Marine captain, and Joel told him that I had just come into some information that perhaps he should hear. He left me with Chuck, and left. I told Chuck what transpired between the patient and me. He asked me a few questions about the dialogue, and whether or not I thought it was credible. I told him that I simply had no way of knowing, but that I found that it was curious that first of all the patient's communication ability was supposedly impaired but it wasn't, and then that he preferred to communicate with me in English rather than Vietnamese or French, and then the ominous forecast, and then completely shutting down. Chuck then told me to spend some more time with the patient, but not to make it too obvious to him that I was probing him excessively. Now I was concerned.

Did I just happen onto something dangerous?

I didn't go back to the patient until after dinner, his dinner, not mine. This time he was a bit more forthcoming. He told me that his family was actually from Hue, and that he noticed my Vietnamese was with a Hue accent. He complimented me on my French. He kept telling me how thirsty he was, and he hoped the Repose had enough water for him. With the fluidity of this conversation, I felt, so much for him being cognitively impaired. It seemed that in spite of his head injury, his cognition was intact, although I couldn't be one hundred percent sure. He still could be delusional. It was then that he told me that his brother was still in the North, and that he thought that his brother had mixed feelings about communism, Ho Chi Minh, and U. S. involvement in his country. In other words, his brother might have been signaling him about another, perhaps specific or imminent, attack. This could have been just to save his brother or it might be reflecting a signal to our side, since clearly the patient was a South Vietnamese official. In reviewing the patients chart once again, it was more obvious that his head injury was not as devastating as was documented. It occurred to me that maybe this was an admission to a place where he could not be seen as passing on information to the Americans. And, that could also explain his being in an American G.I. bar in Saigon, again being unusual for a government official. So, I passed that information onto Chuck later. Chuck then said, "Doc, we might need you in country sooner than later."

He called me "Doc" and not Tom or Bac Si. Something was up, and I was soon to find out.

CHAPTER 14

The next day

I had been on the Repose less than forty-eight hours, and already my tour here looked like it was going to be cut short, shorter than a Temporary Additional Duty, TDY. My suspicions grew, almost immediately, when the overhead page announced, "Lieutenant Staffieri, to the bridge. Lieutenant Staffieri to the bridge."

I hurried to Neurology and Psychiatry where I found Joel. I didn't know how to get to the bridge. I would assume that if I were going to meet with Captain Baker again, it would be in his office, and I knew how to get there. I knew that Captain Baker was not really the captain of the ship. As a Naval vessel, a Captain of the line, regular Navy with a star on his dress blue uniform sleeve as opposed to an oak leaf with an acorn on it, signifying Medical Corps, would be the main person on the bridge. In this case both the ship Captain and Captain Baker would be there. Joel told me how to get to the bridge and off I went, hurriedly.

Two Marine guards were stationed outside of the bridge. They both saluted me simultaneously, and opened the door for me and ushered me in. Since this was clearly business, I stood at attention and said, "Lieutenant Staffieri reporting as ordered, sir."

He looked up, and then excused two of his fellow medical officers, and introduced me to the actual ship captain of the Repose, Captain Robert Collins, USN, and said, "At ease Tom, and have a seat. We have a change in your orders. I alerted CINCPAC, Commander in Chief, Pacific, as to your talk with your patient Mr. Ngyen Diem, yesterday. Since he was not technically your patient, there was no violation of confidentiality, etcetera. You are now ordered in country, to Saigon, where you will receive further orders. I am sorry son, but I fear you are going into the belly of the beast."

I had only been aboard for such a short time, and was beginning to like being a part of this angel of mercy, as I recalled that it had been called for several decades, even back to the Korean War, The Angel of the Orient. Captain Baker told me that he would let me now when I would be detached and deployed. This would depend on further orders from CINCPAC, the Commander-in-Chief of the Pacific. His guess was that I would be leaving in a few days, but reiterated that it was merely his guess. In the meantime I could either see patients with Joel, or try to get any personal things done, like writing letters or working on any articles I might be writing.

Or, as he went on to say, "Listen to some Vietnamese language tapes."

I chose the latter, but thought I might also brush up on my French, and so I would listen to those tapes as well. Actually with French, I would typically listen to record albums of French singers. It seemed the sultry love songs in French helped me learn the language much easier, perhaps in the hopes of meeting and wooing a beautiful Eurasian girl, who was of the beautiful mixture of her French and Vietnamese gene pool. I saw pictures of the young women of Viet Nam, wearing their ao dai's, those tunic style dresses with slits up the sides, over flowing silk trousers. That exotic look, and those lithe figures, well how could that image not appeal to a young man so far from home? And that was me, a young man so far from home, getting anxious about what would come next.

Chuck Caldwell came to my quarters and knocked. I bid him to enter and he came in and sat down. "Chuck, what's up?"

He smiled that passive-aggressive smile he displayed when we flew out to the Repose. Clearly something was on his mind and he knew something about what my new orders might be.

"What's my future like, Chuck?" I asked. "I know you know something."

He said, "My guess is that we will be heading out within the next couple or three days."

"We?" I asked.

He then proceeded to tell me his thoughts on what was likely to transpire and why. He told me about an intercepted communiqué between two major North Vietnamese Army companies south of the DMZ that indicated that some major assault was planned within the next two weeks. The interaction I had had with Mr. Diem supported the assessment that something was in the offing. It sounded like a possible simultaneous strike including Da Nang, Saigon, and the Tan Son Nhut air base. This was major, and we needed to find out when and how, and how many troops would be making the assault. The information was deemed reliable, but information changed day-by-day, and actually hour-by-hour. We simply had to get more intel about this apparently major assault. The question I asked myself was how did I fit into the equation.

So I asked Chuck, "What does all of this have to do with me? I am a Navy Psychologist. What can I do about a military assault? Hell, I don't even typically carry a weapon."

The next couple of days were pretty much routine in terms of clinical work. There were patients to be seen so they would be sent on to their future recovery destination. I spent some time with the child who was napalm burned. I also spent time with patient Diem. We talked less and less in English, and more and more, first in French and later Vietnamese. And, he corrected me in both, politely of course, and only after he asked if he could. In the little time left that we would spend talking, he opened up more and more about being torn between his being from the Hue, and his rise to some prominence in the government of South Viet Nam. He also spoke of his brother, who he described as a patriot, but a misinformed one, and who had remained in Hue, and then went North. He was quite candid, it seemed, about keeping in touch with his brother, in spite of their apparent differences in political philosophies. Either this guy was feeding me a bunch of crap or he was caught in a family and political dilemma. I read about this phenomenon in our own history books. Brother against brother. A house divided. It was called The Civil War, and that is what we had here, over nine thousand miles from Gettysburg.

I was convinced that although he had an inkling about something imminent about to happen, whether it was directly from his brother, who clearly was either VC or NVA, or whether it was because that is what happens in war, or that as a government official you are privy to intelligence findings, he didn't know what that was. He seemed legitimately concerned about the little girl who was burned, and even offered to help in anyway he could. That offer, too, I found to be sincere.

Three days later my new orders came down. Chuck brought them to me. We would be flying out the next day, to Saigon. I thought to myself, going to Saigon is not exactly going into the belly of the beast, or is it. I ran into Captain Baker as he was making surgical rounds. I forgot that he was a surgeon as well as the chief medical officer of the Repose. He chatted with me and asked if I had received my orders from Captain Caldwell, and when I told him that I had, he shook my hand and wished me good luck and safety, and hoped that I would be able to spend more time on the Repose after my "mission." After my "mission?" I thought, what the hell did that mean?

Joel caught up with me and asked whether or not I had received new orders and whether I had heard anything else. I told him that yes, I had received new orders and that I would be leaving the next day and heading to Saigon. I told him that I would be on a new "mission," but didn't know what that really was, and asked him if he had any idea.

He just nodded and said that he had a good guess. He thought that given my language skills that I might be asked to help question some VC prisoners. Certainly they had other military, and civilian personnel for that matter, who were fluent, perhaps even more so than I, in Vietnamese, but given that I was a psychologist, and had particular skills in dealing with stress that......and he just let the rest of his speculation trail off. He had to rush off, but I called after him and asked him to pay some attention to the little girl who was severely burned and to Diem, who I thought might be fragile or potentially volatile. He assured me that he would, and that we could discuss the cases a bit more in the mess hall, when we had dinner later. I figured that I was pretty much finished on the ward, so I headed back to my quarters, where I would at least begin to pack my things, not that I had all that much stuff with me. I had put up a couple of pictures on my desk when I unpacked, trying to make home away from home a little more like home. I had not unpacked everything I brought with me, so I thought I had better at least let my clothes air out a bit, so I unpacked them and would re-pack them after I had dinner. At least they wouldn't be musty when I reported in, to whomever I would be reporting into, in Saigon. My orders read for me to report to Commanding Officer, Joint Military Command Saigon, whoever that might be. I needed to travel in the morning and report in by 1530. I needed to check with Chuck about when he would be flying me there. I wondered if anyone else was coming with. I couldn't believe that this flight was solely for me, remembering that we brought a medical box with us on the way out to the Repose. Putting that out of my mind I began reminiscing again. Back to Bethesda, back to Georgetown, and ultimately back to Milwaukee. Ah, to turn back time. I really didn't want to be here, and I was soon to learn that there were other places where I didn't want to be even more.

CHAPTER 15

Flying Into The Beast

The next morning I packed the rest of my duffle and then went to the mess area and had breakfast. There seemed to be many more people there for breakfast than the days before. Maybe I was getting paranoid but several of them glanced at me, rather than on previous days, when no one really paid any attention to me. I thought, my "mission" therefore might not be all that top secret, and if people knew about it, it couldn't be dangerous or secret. Ah yes, naïveté'. One's mind really does use rationalization as a defense mechanism, as Freud postulated. It turns out that all they really knew was that I had been sent to the Repose a few days ago, saw patients briefly, and was leaving again. Was I getting an R&R already? That couldn't be, unless as I had heard, on occasion, prior to a dangerous mission people were granted an R&R, sort of like a "last meal." Since I wasn't going on R&R, I felt a little better that Command probably wasn't thinking that I needed a "last meal." Joel met me, as I was finishing breakfast. He brought his cup of coffee over to the table.

"Hi Tom. Packed and ready to go? I wish you could stay longer. I could sure use the help, and the patients you have seen all seem to like you. And, I heard that a couple of the nurses do too. I really hope that as soon as they are through with you in county, that they will ship you back here. Maybe they would let you finish your tour aboard the Repose. Anyway, Tom, I wish you well and God's speed. Keep your head down, ok?"

We shook hands and off he went, back to see more patients. He really was a dedicated physician. I was getting a little antsy, so I looked for Chuck Caldwell, but instead saw Paul Reynolds, my corpsman friend.

"Hey Pauly, come on over and join me for coffee. I am leaving in an hour or so. Glad I had a chance to see you before I left. I'm not sure where I will be going after Saigon. Maybe here or maybe back to Pearl."

He said, "Not to worry Bac Si, I'm going to Saigon with you."

I was surprised, but actually glad, that Paul would be making the trip to Da Nang with us, but actually he said Saigon. That meant he would be probably doing something more than picking up another medical box. I didn't query him about that and merely said that I was glad to have company, and that if there was time, I would buy him a Ba Moui Ba when we landed.

He smiled and said, "Sure, Doc."

I got the distinct feeling that Paul, too, knew something more than he was letting on, and probably more about my orders, than I did. My suspicions were heightened when Chuck came to the table and Paul greeted him in Vietnamese, and not merely with "Xin Chao," but also asking him in fluent Vietnamese, what time we needed to take off, was everything we needed on board the helicopter, and somewhat ominously if Bac Si here was going to pack a revolver. Perhaps he forgot that I understood, or maybe he was saying that for my benefit. My suspicion was now turning into paranoia.

I turned to Paul and said, "You know I understood everything you said, don't know? Why would you think I needed to pack heat? You know that I am a psychologist don't you? You do know that I don't shoot people, I talk to them?"

Both Paul and Chuck merely smiled.

Paul said, "Sorry Bac Si. Yes I do know that you understand, and yes

I do know that you are a psychologist, and yes I do know that you don't pack heat, as you say, and that you talk to people. Just know that how you talk to some people just might need a little emphasis."

What in the hell did he mean by that. I just let it go, though. On one hand I hoped that he would elaborate a bit, and on the other hand hoping that he wouldn't. Frankly, now I was getting a little more apprehensive. What was in store for me in Saigon? What was in store for me in general? Maybe I wasn't getting a little more apprehensive. Maybe I was getting scared.

Chuck looked at his watch and said, "Tom, Paul, it is time we load up and take off. Do either of you need any help with your gear? Mine is already on board. I had to put some medical stuff on board at bit earlier. The Captain wanted to send some medical supplies over to the dispensary in Saigon, probably for one of his doctor friends over there. They tend to run out of some of the basics when some of the wounded are brought there first, before they might be sent out here to the Repose or someplace else. Captain Baker sends stuff over, whenever he can, and I think that it generally "off the record." He really is a good guy."

I thought to myself that it was interesting that medical supplies would need to flow from the hospital ship to a ground facility where presumably they would receive supplies directly from CONUS and then supply the hospital ship, and not the other way around. I would come to learn all about how some supplies tend to disappear in war, and then turn up on the black market.

I picked up my gear, said goodbye to some of the nurses I met briefly, and boarded the helicopter, where Chuck and Paul were waiting. As soon as I boarded, Chuck started the engine and the huge rotor began turning. I put on my headphones, which were somewhat noise cancelling, as well as a way to hear and communicate with anyone on board, and most importantly with the pilot. We received our clearance and began to lift off. It is always a treat to experience lifting off in a helicopter, more so than in an airplane. In spite of the headphones, however, the noise of a helicopter is consuming. It is like the muffler sound of a motorcycle, but not as tinny. The headphones do make a difference though. As we lifted off, I again marveled at the size of this floating hospital. Even as we moved further away and reached a distance of a half-mile, the Repose still loomed large. We approached the coast and approached the airfield at Da Nang, but we kept flying. We were obviously bypassing Da Nang, which actually surprised me, and headed west toward Saigon. I thought that we would at least touch down in Da Nang, if only for fuel or supplies or carrying some equipment or supplies to Saigon. Flying back into Viet Nam was a little different from when we flew out of Viet Nam. No one was shooting at us this time. So far, so good.

An hour after we lifted off from the aft deck of the Repose, we approached Saigon. Passing over some of the old, Colonial French buildings, interspersed with shrines to Buddha, was a sight to behold. I thought to myself that it was a shame that there was a war going on down there. But, there was, in fact, a war going on down there, but not only down there, but throughout this beautiful land, this beautiful part of the world. Viet Nam was definitely the "Pearl of the Orient."

We were cleared to land, and Chuck put us down relatively softly. He really was a good pilot. I sensed, more and more, however, that he was much more than just a pilot. I also began thinking that about my friend, the corpsman. I had heard early on about C.I.A., Central Intelligence Agency, involvement in Southeast Asia. Could Chuck and Paul be C.I.A.? After thinking about that for a moment, I dismissed that. Clearly they were military, just like me. Well, maybe not just like me.

Saigon was hot, and humid, and busy, and teaming. We landed at the airport and of course there was military everywhere, including the "White Mice," the South Vietnamese military styled police. They were called "White Mice" because of the white helmets they wore. Actually they were fairly efficient, even though typically the U.S. military personnel viewed them with some disdain and even scorn. We were ostensibly there to help these people but clearly some of us were not respecting them. And, in some ways, rightly so. It became clear that we were fighting their fight. And, as in probably every war man has ever fought, war opportunists were present. G.I.'s, I learned, were frequently ripped off. In this war another variable was present, often times you could not distinguish friend from foe. Perhaps this was the feeling of Rebels and Yankees, in our own Civil War. Friend and foe simply looked alike then, and now.

Somehow Chuck had a jeep waiting for us at the tarmac. He got in it and said for Paul and I to load our gear and a small box in the back of the helicopter. We dutifully obeyed. Chuck really did convey authority, or at least someone who knew what he was doing. Clearly I didn't. Know what I was doing, that is. I thought I could use a beer, and I said that to Chuck.

He said "Sure Doc, we'll stop and get one before you have to report. We have some time. Not to worry."

We pulled up in front of this seedy looking bar. He turned off the jeep and got out and walked into the bar.

He looked back and said, "Well, do you need an invitation?"

I asked him about our bags, mine in particular. I felt that my bag held everything I owned, at least here in Viet Nam, and I didn't want to have it ripped off. I knew how things were back in Gary. You just didn't leave an open car with anything in it. If you did, nothing would be left, and possibly even the tires. Chuck assured me that he knew this bar and that someone would come out right away and watch our stuff. I didn't believe him, nor would I heed his direction to leave my gear. Hey, I knew about Gary. He didn't. So, I took my duffle bag with me. He laughed as I sat down at a table and put my bag on the floor, next to my chair. I thought I knew why he laughed, but I was wrong.

A moment later a bar girl came to the table and sat next to me. She kicked my bag out of the way and said, "Buy me drink G.I.?"

I looked at her and told her in Vietnamese, "Khong," which she understood by my inflection as meaning get the hell out of here.

She left and muttered, in English, "ass-hole."

We ordered a round of "33 biere," and quickly downed them and ordered another round. They were cold, and actually pretty good. They were so good, in fact, that I did not compare them to "The Beer that made Milwaukee famous."

Chuck laughed and said, "Bac Si, didn't you like my gift? I'm sure she liked you. She would love you beaucoup."

Unbelievable, I thought. I am back in college.

We finished our beers and it was time to head out. I still had an hour to report in. Again, to whom, I had no clue, but I was sure Chuck and his faithful companion Paul, would get me there, and to the right person. We traversed the bustling streets of Saigon. It was as busy as Washington, D.C., only on a smaller scale, and by smaller scale I also meant the people. They all were so small. I didn't pay too much attention to the men. The young women were beautiful, and in their ao dai's, I could see why I had heard that the American G.I.'s were so taken by these young women. Most of them appeared so prim and proper, not like the bar girls, many of whom, I later learned, were banging American G.I.'s during the day, and Victor Charlie, the VC, at night, including the "gift" Chuck sent over to me and who would love me "too beaucoup."

We reached the military compound and the Marine guards saluted Chuck. Clearly they could see his rank insignia, and perhaps mine as well. I was sitting in the front of the jeep with Chuck while Paul was in the back seat with the bags and the mysterious medical box. I had wondered why I was not privy to what was in the box, and still wondered why medical supplies needed to be ferried back and forth from the Repose to land facilities, especially since they were being conveyed in both directions. But, I figured, it was not my business, so I just let it go. Yet, the box intrigued me, and it appeared fairly light. What kind of medical supplies could be in the box, and why so light? It couldn't be equipment because it would have to be heavier. So, I really couldn't get it completely out of my mind. After Chuck saluted the guards we drove into the compound and drove for about ten minutes, taking left turns and right turns, and seeming to go in circles. Navigation was not one of my strong suits. We came to a compound within the compound. This compound was surrounded by concertina wire, with what appeared to be razor blades at the top. Where in the hell was I? I am a Navy shrink. What is this all about? Chuck showed his identification to another set of Marine guards. The guards came over to me and asked, no demanded, my identification. I produced my military I.D., and then tried to reach back to my duffle to get my orders.

One guard pointed his rifle at me and said, "Sir, stop. I will get whatever is in your bag."

The other guard also had pointed his rifle at me, and the first guard took my bag, opened it, and found that all it contained was my clothes, some pictures, and my folder with my orders. Chuck then explained that we were there for me to report in to Colonel Jackson Frey. How did Chuck know the name of the officer to whom I was to report? This was getting more and more curious, and ominous. With that, the Marine guards saluted and waved us into the compound. They apparently didn't pay much attention to Paul, in the back seat. Again, curious. We stopped in front of a fairly nondescript building, more of a Quonset hut than a building. There was another Marine guard, but he was standing in front of the door rather than to the side of it.

He recognized Chuck and said, "Good afternoon Captain Caldwell, sir."

He opened the door for us, and we stepped in. The air conditioning was refreshing, after the heat and humidity of Saigon. The helicopter ride provided a great breeze, but as soon as we landed our uniforms became soaked with perspiration within ten minutes. I stopped and let the air conditioning cool me and hopefully dry my perspiration soaked uniform. I wanted to look somewhat presentable to my new commanding officer, whoever that might be.

Colonel Jackson Frey stepped out of his office and came forward towards us. He was wearing his marine camouflage uniform, with his full bird colonel insignia on his collar. Tall and erect, he stood six feet tall, and could have been the poster image for the Marine Corps officer.

Chuck didn't salute but stood at attention and greeted his superior, with "Good afternoon, sir."

Colonel Frey extended his hand and said, "Good to see you Chuck. I see you brought our shrink, and his corpsman. Have you briefed him yet?"

I thought, "Briefed him? On what?"

"No sir, I thought it would be best if you did the briefing, and that he heard it from you. Colonel this is Lieutenant Staffieri, and of course you know Reynolds."

I noticed that he referred to Paul by his last name, as in the military enlisted personnel are always referred to by their last names, unless they are senior enlisted, such as a Navy Chief Petty Officer or a Marine Gunnery, or "Gunny" Sergeant.

The Colonel said, "Yes, of course I know Paul. Welcome back son."

It appears that when you are a Colonel you can break protocol and use first names pretty much whenever you'd like. He shook my hand first, and bid me welcome, and then shook Paul's hand. He turned and walked into his office and we dutifully followed.

"Have a seat gentlemen. We are here to discuss a mission that we will launch in three days. This mission can potentially save a great many lives, civilians as well as Marines. It is imperative that we are successful. The fact that the three of you are fluent in Vietnamese, and that you, Tom, have a background in stress and stress management, gives us a significant advantage."

I noticed that he referred to me by my first name, with again military protocol apparently being discretionary for this commanding officer.

"Chuck, did you bring the medical box?"

Chuck nodded and said, "Yes sir, I did. It is in the jeep. A Marine is guarding it, with our gear, so I know it is secure."

They both smiled, since they both knew that the Marine guard, and virtually any Marine guard, would defend his post or his charge with his life. That is the nature of the Marine Corps, "The Few, The Proud, The Marines." So, our gear, but seemingly more importantly, the medical box, was secure.

Colonel Frey told Paul to go out and bring in the medical box. In the meantime he offered Chuck and me something cold to drink. I declined, still feeling a bit full from the beer earlier. He asked if I had, in fact, tried the "33," and I told him that I had, and found it not bad. It turns out that he was an Annapolis graduate, and said that the "33" reminded him of National Bohemian beer, back in Annapolis, after graduation of course. When Paul came back in, the Colonel told him to put the box on his desk, and asked him if he wanted something cold to drink, but Paul, too, respectfully declined. The supposed medical box was like the elephant in the room. Everyone could see it, but no one either wanted or could talk about it. The Colonel asked each of us about our respective health and stamina. He asked me how far I could run and if I felt I was in good shape. He suggested that I hydrate myself well, especially in the jungle. He asked if I had any significant allergies or health issues or if I needed to take medications. I told him that I thought that I was in great shape, having played sports all of my life, and having taken up running during graduate school. He assured me that I would not have to run a distance race, but stamina was important. Again, I was wondering why I was here, and why was he asking about my physical status. After all I was a psychologist, not a Marine.

Then he got to it.

"Tom, I know all of this seems confusing to you. Why have I asked for a psychologist out here? Why one who speaks Vietnamese and French, and why one who is an expert in stress and stress management? Why a concern about stamina, when clearly as a Naval Officer you didn't have to go through the rigors of a Marine Boot Camp? I have in fact, studied your personnel record thoroughly, and I have made phone calls checking on you. I have talked with the Chief of the Medical Service Corps, the Chief of Psychology at BuMed, the Bureau of Medicine and Surgery, and the Chiefs of Psychology and Psychiatry at Bethesda. They all sang your praises, and they all described you not only as an exceptional Naval Officer, an excellent clinician, and excellent psychologist, and a patriot, but they also all said that you were a common sense guy, who could improvise on a situation, a stressful situation, with common sense. That is what I need out here. I have a mission that is critical. We have lost way too many men, not only valuable men, but Marines. I am equally concerned with the civilians we were sent here to defend, and liberate from the perils of the communist North, but I am most concerned about my men, United States Marines. We are fighting a war here, as well as another war, six thousand miles away, back home. And, you might be asked to do, nay have to do, some things that you would never have thought you might have to do as a psychologist. You joined the Navy and assumed that you would be a non-combatant, and in essence and in fact, you are and will remain so. There are however situations that may arise, that might make you reassess your ability to remain non-combatant. I hope it never comes to that, but out here, in this jungle war, we have to expect the unexpected. I do hope that the assessment of you being a common sense person is accurate. I am counting on it. You will have two of my finest under your leadership, your psychological expertise leadership. They, of course will have tactical leadership as well as protective leadership throughout the mission. Are you clear about that? The three of you, Chuck, Paul, and you are going on a mission on the other side of the Cu Chi tunnels. Have you heard of them?"

CHAPTER 16

Learning About The Mission

O f course I had heard about the tunnels of Cu Chi. Those were the elaborate tunnels used by the Viet Cong to first confuse, avoid, and then attack the French, when France was trying to colonize Viet Nam. The Cu Chi tunnel system was begun during the colonial war against the French, but was then refined when the Americans arrived. And, ironically, one of the largest United States Army bases in Viet Nam, Cu Chi, was built directly on top of the tunnel system of the Viet Cong.

Cu Chi was actually a district of Saigon, and before the war, it had a thriving population of over three hundred thousand residents. During the war, however, there were less than one hundred thousand people living there. It was not, however, the residents of that area who were the issue. It was the population below Cu Chi that was significant. The tunnel system under Cu Chi, which actually stretched from approximately twenty miles outside of Saigon proper, all the way to the Cambodian border, probably rivaling the New York City Subway system. It was learned that a tunnel system of about one hundred and fifty miles existed within the Cu Chi district alone. Some of these tunnels turned out to be several stories deep. In those tunnels there were living facilities, storage areas, weapons manufacturing sections, kitchens, command centers, and even field hospitals. These tunnels facilitated communication and movement between Viet Cong areas and personnel. This way there were able to move, communicate and strike at South Vietnamese and American interests and troops. Surprise attacks against U.S. forces were launched from these tunnels, including attacks directly on U.S. bases, under which these tunnels were dug over a twenty-five year period. These tunnels actually began being dug in the middle to late 1940's, by the Viet Minh, the precursors of the Viet Cong, even before the Franco-Viet Nam War. However, it was during both wars, the one with the French and later the one with the Americans, that the tunnels of Cu Chi became strategic bases for the Viet Cong to infiltrate, sabotage and smuggle intelligence agents into Saigon. We learned that during my internship year, in 1968, the Tet Offensive was, in fact, developed and launched from the tunnels of Cu Chi. The Tet Offensive was basically launched on the evening of January 31, 1968, during the Vietnamese celebration of the Lunar New Year, when the Viet Cong broke the unofficial cease fire of that national, both North and South, celebration. That offensive, and the North Vietnamese attack on Khe Sanh, which was a prelude to the Tet Offensive, and which was in the DMZ, the Demilitarized Zone, are said to be major turning points in the war. With these assaults planned in the tunnels of Cu Chi, it was obvious that those tunnels were extremely important. Attempts to clear out these tunnels have had mixed results. When German Shepherd dogs were sent into the tunnels, they were sometimes maimed by booby traps, or thrown off scent when the VC used American soap or uniforms of captured or killed American G.I.'s to evade the dogs. The tunnels were dangerously peppered with booby-traps, including grenades, punji sticks, which were sharpened bamboo stalks usually dipped in urine or feces, so as to cause significant infection. Poisonous snakes which were tethered in crevices, so that they would readily strike at an unsuspecting American soldier. These snakes, kraits, were some of the most poisonous snakes in the world. Their venom could kill a man within minutes. In spite of those dangers, there was a certain group of American soldiers who would go down in these tunnels to pursue the enemy, and risk the perils of danger. They were called "tunnel rats." Amazingly, these were volunteer specialists who would do that dangerous work. I would call them clinically "crazy."

I did know the history of the tunnels of Cu Chi, and their importance, but for the life of me I had no clue why or how I would be involved with them, or them with me. Colonel Frey soon enlightened me.

"Tom, I am sending you, Chuck and Paul here, out to Cu Chi. We understand, from various sources, including your Mr. Diem, who you treated on the Repose, and who gave you some information supposedly from his brother, that something major was afoot. We simply cannot have another Tet Offensive or another Khe Sahn. It turns out that your Mr. Diem's brother is a high-ranking North Vietnamese Army General. We are not sure if either, or both of them are reliable, credible, a turncoat, or what. We have to find out about them, as well as whether something major is on the horizon or imminent. I am not going to lose more men. We will do everything we can. You will do everything you can. Understand?"

Colonel Frey's eyes became even more steely than they first appeared to me. This guy was really gung ho, and not just Marine gung ho, but an angry and frustrated gung ho. I believed him when he said that he was not going to lose more men. He was the consummate leader, the kind most men would follow into hell.

All I could say was "Yes, sir" in the best military way a direct commission officer without any formal military training could muster.

I still had no clue what I was being asked, no, ordered to do. The plan was, however, unfolding.

The elephant in the room was still looming in the room, the medical box. After a long minute of silence, Chuck spoke.

"Sir, are we going to take the medical box with us this time? Since Tom is here we might be able to use it. I don't think anyone has had a chance to talk with him about it, any of it. Do you want me to brief him on it? Pauly here can do it, and maybe shed a little more medical light on it. I don't think Lieutenant Commander Rosen had a chance to talk with him about it, since Tom here wasn't on the Repose very long."

Now I was starting to get anxious again. What was I getting into? Fear began to replace anxiety.

Colonel Frey was sensing my anxiety and fear. Apprehension was probably a more accurate description of what I was feeling.

He walked over to me and put his hand on my shoulder and said, "Son, you will do fine. I know that there might be some things you have not been prepared to see or face, but I know that you will rise to the occasion. You will not be asked to do anything that is not in the best interest of your country. You will not be asked to betray your moral standards. You will, however, be asked to utilize your common sense in dealing with the enemy, nothing more, nothing less. You are going into this mission a good man, and you will come out a good man. Do you hear me?"

I was at least somewhat reassured by his bolstering speech. Ah, the power of persuasion.

We discussed hypotheticals when dealing with the enemy. We discussed classified positions and troop strength, both theirs and ours. And we finally discussed the mission, at least the theoretical mission. Colonel Frey was quite candid that our foray into trying to capture high ranking enemy soldiers, whether they were Viet Cong, or North Vietnamese Army (NVA) Regulars, was problematic at best, but hopeful, and quite frankly necessary. All that our commanders knew was that it was imperative to know what major enemy assault or offensive was imminent. Our troops depended on that intelligence. And it appeared that Chuck, Pauly and I were the ones charged to get that intel.

After Ho Chi Minh, the titular head of North Viet Nam, died in September of 1969, there was some reported confusion in leadership of the North. Immediately following Ho Chi Minh's death, North Viet Nam was run essentially by committee, with the new leader being Le Duan. But that was all it was. Reported. Some of the intel the South had received was becoming obviously disinformation, aimed at confusing the South, but more importantly, the Americans. So, we needed accurate, first hand, intelligence. We needed to know about leadership and battle planning of our enemy. We needed words from the horse's mouth, so to speak. It looked like our trio of merry men was to get that intel. Why in God's name did I learn Vietnamese?

"The three of you are going to fly up to about 5 klicks from the Cambodian border, and from there you will meet up with some Montagnards who know the area well. There you will survey until you come across a reported company of NVA regulars. They are supposed to be led by your Mr. Diem's brother, General Nuc Diem. He is one of the NVA's leading generals, and he has always insisted on leading his troops into battle. He is older than his brother, and was leading troops, even as a young man, against the French. General Diem knows what we need to know. Your mission is to get into his brain and get that information. Tom, you are going to be crucial in this mission, so don't get killed or caught."

I said to myself, "Killed or caught?" Did he just say to not get killed or caught? In the parlance of the G.I., this is FUBAR, the acronym for Fucked Up Beyond All Recognition. I was still wondering what I was expected to do, although some things were becoming increasingly evident. Somehow my psychological training and my language skills were intertwined for this mission. I was guessing how, and soon found out.

"Tom, Chuck here is a combat trained Marine as well as a pilot, and other things. He will locate and capture General Diem. Intel so far has learned that the General is headquartered in one of the tunnels that are near the Cambodian border. When you find him, Paul here will sedate him. You will interrogate him there in the field, and if necessary, use the medical box. General Diem will then be brought back here, and we will hold him as long as necessary. We will debrief you for the information you extracted from the General, and coordinate that information with other intel we have, and therefore hopefully aborting any imminent attack or major offensive the enemy has planned. We will then launch an immediate pre- emptive counter attack. Do you understand?"

I nodded, knowing that I still didn't understand fully what my parameters were, but was certainly suspecting. I still didn't know the significance of the medical box, and why no one was addressing what was in it.

CHAPTER 17

The Medical Box

"LSD? LSD is in that fucking box? Unbelievable. What in the hell are we supposed to do with LSD? Get High?"

This was not at all what I expected. And then, Pauly told me that there was Marijuana in the "medical" box, as well. Now I knew I was in the wrong place. I needed to be back at Bethesda, not out here on the other side of the world, with a bunch of mind-altering drugs. I wouldn't mind if someone smoked a joint, but LSD, if nothing else, caused flashbacks, and who knew when those flashbacks might occur. This was FUBAR! Of course the psychiatrists back on the psychiatry unit at Bethesda had their own psychotropic medications, which were legitimately mind altering. But this? FUBAR! Granted, I knew that a significant number of our troops out here used drugs, primarily marijuana, but this scenario was unbelievable.

LSD, lysergic acid diethylamide, is a drug popular in a sub culture wanting to "drop out," as Timothy Leary, a proponent of this drug, suggested youth do. It brought on vivid auditory and visual hallucinations, and paradoxically was thought to be a cure for schizophrenia. So did Linus Pauling's work that suggested that vitamin C could also cure schizophrenia. I was smart enough to question both of those theories. I also knew that the hippocampus, the part of the brain usually most associated with learning and memory, was more often than not the part of the brain most affected by LSD. After a typical LSD "trip" a person who ingested the drug would not remember much about the "trip," as the hippocampus acts to protect memory and the encoding of information stored. Basically, that meant that a person having ingested LSD, could reveal information and then not have a recollection of what he revealed. Ah ha! That is what the plan was. To get General Diem to reveal troop movements and offensive plans. And the marijuana? Well, that would help him mellow out, and put him in such a relaxed state that he would cooperate with the information retrieval even more easily. What a plan. And, using "data" gleaned from "street pharmacy" findings. Again, I thought, Unbelievable.

So, I supposed, Chuck would be in charge of the locating and capture of General Diem. Pauly would somehow get him to smoke a little pot and then get him to ingest a tab of acid, the LSD, and then I would handle the interrogation. From an ethical point of view, since Pauly was a corpsman and had not professional affiliation, he would be off the hook. I, on the other hand, had somewhat of an ethical issue about participating in possible tortuous interrogations. That was still being debated by the professional psychological and psychiatric organizations. But rationalization helped here. Would this really be torture? Maybe it could be viewed as "enhanced interrogation." And, I was a military psychologist, in the middle of a war, and was anything really being done to harm an individual. That would be the question. I guess that bridge would be crossed, if and when we came to it. We might not even be able to find, much less capture the General. Still, I knew that I would obsess about it until the situation confronted itself. I had studied about the various brainwashing techniques during the Korean War. Were we going to make a "Manchurian Candidate" after we got our information?

Colonel Frey must have been assessing my reaction to all this new information, and finally said, "Lieutenant Staffieri, I have pre-empted your ethical concern. I not only ran this by Lieutenant Commander Rosen, but I was able to reach BuMed, and spoke both with the heads of Psychiatry and Psychology there. They both gave the green light on this, especially since you would not directly be administering the drugs. Humane interrogation is acceptable under the Geneva Convention, and the Rules of War."

I thought "Rules of War? Rules of friggin' war?"

All I could say was "Yes sir, thank you sir."

I must say, however, that I did feel somewhat better with Colonel Frey's reassurance and running it by others, more senior, in the field.

He then said, "Gentlemen, we will meet at 0715 tomorrow, and go over the last minute details and the latest intel on the whereabouts of our General Diem. Now go and get something to eat, and try to relax a bit. Dismissed."

As the three of us turned around and began to exit, I started to say something, but Chuck nudged me to be quiet. I wanted to ask more about the mission, but I heeded Chuck's nudge.

As soon as we were out of the office and out of ear shot, I said, "Chuck, Paul, can you guys please explain to me what the hell is going on. Are we going into "Indian Country" all alone? Are we going to have at least a company of Marines with us? How do we get back from visiting General Diem? How are you planning to capture him, especially if he is in a tunnel surrounded by a battalion, company or whatever? How am I supposed to get information from him? What is all this shit with LSD and pot? Tell me I'm dreaming, and that this is just some horrible nightmare. Tell me that I actually have orders to go back to Bethesda, tomorrow morning. Please tell me something."

They both looked at me with a serious look and then Chuck said, "Sorry Tommy, it's for real. Sorry I couldn't tell you anything before, and sorry I couldn't prepare you for this, but now it is what it is, and you will be fine. Everyone has the utmost confidence in you, and I know you will get the intel we need. Don't worry about the other stuff, Paul and I will take care of everything else, and just as importantly, we will take care of you."

He said that with such conviction, that it actually put me somewhat at ease.

Then Paul said, "Let's go get a beer and something to eat. Who knows when we will eat something decent anytime soon, or have a beer."

So we passed the Marine guards, got into our jeep, and out of the compound we rode.

Chuck then said, "After we get something to eat, we'll get back to the base, and go to the Officer's Club for another beer. Then we'll get you a weapon, Tom, and get us to our respective quarters. We can talk more there, and then call it a night. We can get up early and get over to the Colonel's by 0715, for the final briefing, ok?" Chuck was clearly in charge, and looked like he had a plan, at least for the immediate time. I nodded in agreement, as did Paul.

But, I was thinking, "A weapon? I need a weapon? Unbelievable!"

We pulled up in front of the old Majestic Hotel, which was a beautiful building of colonial architecture, and had one of the best roof top bars in the city. The three of us decided that we just could not deal with a cheaper and seedier bar, teeming with bar girls bothering you for a little "boom boom," every five minutes. So the Majestic was the clear choice. It was elegant, not crowded, and catered to high ranking South Vietnamese, American officers, and now us. It was quiet when we entered, with only soft piano music playing in the background. Chuck was greeted by the hostess, and we were shown to a table by the window, over looking the river as well as the city lights. A beautiful waitress, dressed in the traditional ao dai, came and took our order. There was no attempt at getting us to buy anything other than what we wanted, and in this case, a round of "33" beer. That beer was actually starting to taste pretty good to me. When the beers were brought to the table, we thanked the waitress and told her that we were going to run a tab.

She smiled and said, "Cam on," which was a sweet sounding

"thank you."

When I saw her in the reflection in the window, and drinking the first sip of beer, I had an immediate flashback to college. I was having a beer at the Pfister Hotel, in Milwaukee, with Carolyn. Why was I thinking of that special coed now, eight thousand miles away from where we held hands, looked into each other's eyes, and professed our forever love?

I snapped out of it, when Paul said, "Tom, what are you thinking about? You are smiling, so it must be about home."

Little did he know.

I simply replied, "Oh nothing."

We drank our beers, and I signaled our waitress to bring another round. It was then that Chuck began talking about the mission, and what he knew about the area, how to get to the Cambodian border destination, and what we might encounter. He indicated that unless there were snipers along the way, it should not get too hairy until we got to about ten clicks, about six miles, from our destination. If, in fact, General Diem were there, he would no doubt have at least a platoon with him, and the rest of a company fairly close. In the tunnels more than likely. Of course I was curious as to how we would get the General out of the tunnel, and then try to isolate him so we could get to him and snatch him, and then "turn him on." Chuck did have a plan.

CHAPTER 18

The Plan

"The entire platoon! With LSD? LSD! You want me to turn on an entire platoon of the Viet Cong? FUBAR!"

I was blown away.

"You plan to get an entire platoon, and possibly an entire company, high? You want ME to turn them on? Are you nuts? Just how do you think you, or we, are going to pull that off? I thought turning on the General was a bizarre idea, but turning on a minimum of twelve to fifteen people, and then possibly an entire company of soldiers? Unbelievable!"

Here I had been worried about some possible ethical violation on my part, if somehow I might be complicit in getting one person, the General, to ingest a psychotropic drug. Now I might be complicit in drugging a dozen or more people? What have I gotten myself into? I had no problem asking questions in an interrogation, but the drug part was more than a little problematic for me, even with the assurances Colonel Frey gave me about senior mental health professionals giving their imprimatur.

Chuck then proceeded to tell me all about the Montagnards. Basically the Montagnards were mountain and hill people, in central and northern Viet Nam. Since they were mountain people, which is what the French called them when they were in Indochina. And, ever since then, they were referred to by the French name, Montagnards.

Although the French, when they were in Indochina, French Indochina, called them Montagnards, ethnic Vietnamese called them "Moi," which meant "savages," even though they were anything but savages. They were a peaceful people, and resisted the indoctrination attempts of the communist North, and therefore were treated poorly, if not killed, by the Viet Cong or NVA. Although they had more of an allegiance to the South, they were generally non political, and fiercely independent. They did befriend the American troops, who they felt always treated them well. As a sign of friendship, they frequently presented a G.I. with a brass or silver bracelet. I noticed that Chuck wore one of those bracelets. He obviously knew these people, and was extremely friendly with them. I would soon learn exactly how friendly. Paul knew the story of Chuck's first involvement with the Montagnards. On a previous tour in Viet Nam, Chuck led a platoon of Marines into the Central Highlands. His platoon came under heavy attack, and was surrounded by a company of NVA regulars who had infiltrated beyond the DMZ and were in the Central Highlands. This assault was viewed by a large group of Montagnards, who had benefitted from food and other provisions given to them by other Marines. They saw the Marines under fire and sustaining significant casualties. They knew that they had to do something. They certainly could not attack the NVA, so they took surrounding positions and began blowing horns, and making so much noise and commotion that the NVA thought American reinforcements were coming, and so they subsequently withdrew. When the NVA company left, the Montagnards went in and helped the Americans with their wounded. One of the wounded was 1st Lieutenant Charles Caldwell. The Montagnards witnessed Chuck's bravery. They reported Chuck's bravery under fire, to another detachments of Marines, that was being led by then, Major Jackson Frey. Chuck, I learned had single handedly carried wounded back to shelter, all the time firing his weapon at the enemy. He saved the lives of four out of the five men he carried to safety. He was shot in the shoulder at the same time the man he was carrying was shot in the head. That was the only one of the five men Chuck carried, who died. For that act of bravery, Chuck was awarded a Silver Star. That award was recommended by Major Frey. That Montagnard tribe never forgot his bravery, and also his acknowledging and rewarding their assistance in that battle. He brought them much needed supplies, including medicine and canned food, can opener included. They were henceforth life-long friends.

It turns out that the particular tribe of Montagnards was a target of the VC. And those VC told their NVA brethren about them. The NVA tortured and killed several members of the tribe, at least ones they could find. The Gnards, as they were referred to, knew the land better than the soldiers, of either side. So, they could hide in places no one else could think of. They knew how to blend into the environment, much like a chameleon. If anyone knew about the topography of the area, and where the entrances to the tunnels might be and movement of troops, the Gnards would. They were great to have on our side, and would be a definite plus, if not a necessity, on our mission, as was Chuck.

We continued to talk about our mission, and how it might unfold, possible scenarios, consequences and outcomes. We talked around the worse scenario, us being captured or killed. Wounded would be acceptable, but not captured or killed. I again thought, this is definitely not what I signed up for. I am a psychologist, a non-combatant, and now I am going into battle? I ordered another beer.

CHAPTER 19

BOQ Saigon

After we finished our third beer at the roof top bar of the Majestic, we paid our tab, and bid the waitress and host a good evening "Chao buoi toi."

They bowed politely, but you couldn't help but wonder if they or their family were VC. They gave no indication of it, but you couldn't help but be a little paranoid about that, even in Saigon, or maybe especially in Saigon. But, our fearless leader Chuck seemed to know the people there, so that somewhat allayed my fears. We did munch on some bar food while we were there, so we really weren't hungry. Our bags were seemingly untouched in the jeep, as there was good security at the Majestic, and Chuck seemed to know the security guard who had us park the jeep directly in front of the hotel, in constant plain view of the security guard. Chuck had also, as a precaution, placed some dye packs in strategic locations in and around our bags. They would explode a red dye if moved in a particular way, although not if simply nudged by jeep movement. There was no red dye on the bags, nor inside of them when he looked in each of the three bags. So, we were on our way back to the base, and to the BOQ, where Chuck and I would be staying. Paul would be in the enlisted quarters. He didn't seem to mind not being in "Officer's Country" for the night.

We stopped after we entered the base, and we pulled over and got out of the jeep. We were going to talk a bit more about the plan, the schedule, and what time to meet up the next morning. Paul lit a cigarette, and wanted to go over the plan again, but this time wanting to know more about how we were gong to get to the Montagnards, and how exactly they were going to help us get to General Diem. We all knew that there would also have to be an element of luck involved in our plan. In a crazy way, it was becoming exciting. Crazy but exciting.

Clearly Chuck was going to lead this mission. That was clear from the beginning. Even Colonel Frey seemed to defer to him when he outlined the plan. It was also clear that Colonel Frey and Chuck were, if not the masterminds of this possible folly, certainly had something to do with its hatching. If I stood back and analyzed it, I would have to say that it was truly crazy, and that would be, in fact, my diagnosis. Not of them, but the plan. Well, maybe of them too.

So we talked. I asked if something like this had ever been done before.

Chuck asked, "What, turning a platoon of enemy soldiers and their commanding officer into a bunch of hippies, taking LSD?"

We all laughed, but actually that was what I was thinking. Paul, too, must have been thinking it, because he laughed the hardest. When we stopped laughing and settled down, we discussed the most likely scenario of getting the drugs to, and then into, the enemy. Clearly the water supply, or the food. We had to see where they would come out of the tunnels in order to get their water. If we could find that out, we might have a shot at this crazy scheme. That, Chuck said, was what he was hoping the Montagnards could help us with. Then, we had to discuss how we might be able to snatch the General, out from under the noses of his troops.

We were still not certain as to the timing of this adventure. All we knew was that we were to meet with the Colonel at 0715. So after we dropped Paul off at his quarters, Chuck and I headed over to the BOQ, where we were billeted. We parked the jeep in the lot adjacent to the building, and took out our bags and carried them in. The Filipino steward on duty greeted us and directed us to our respective rooms. They were on the first floor and adjacent to each other. I dropped my bag inside the door of my room, as did Chuck inside his. He asked me to come back to his room after I got situated, and we could talk some more. So, I just washed my face with cold water, and felt a bit more refreshed. I really needed to talk more about this caper we were going on. So, I walked next door to Chuck's room, knocked and walked in when he said to enter. It was then that I noticed his military medals. He had taken out his dress jacket, and all of his medals were on it. And, there it was, with all the others, including a Purple Heart, was the Silver Star. This guy was a real hero. It was then that I felt more secure. As I looked at his medals, he must have noticed and said, "Don't be too secure because of those. I am scared too." That was reassuring yet a bit frightening. I was confident in my leader's ability, and somewhat reassured about his fear too. It is comforting to know that a battle-hardened veteran has the same fear as you, a novice, have.

"Thanks Chuck. I needed to hear that. And yes, I am scared."

He said, "Try not to worry too much, Tom. This really is doable. And, if you can do your part, we will save a lot of lives, a lot of good Marine lives. I know you will do your part. Just know that I will do mine. And Pauly will do his. He is good. The Montagnards are good. They are loyal, and they will do anything to get the NVA out of their mountains."

I actually slept fairly decently that night, although I did wake up finally at 0600. I showered and looked for a place to get a wake up cup of coffee. But that was to no avail. I would have to wait until Chuck and I would pick up Paul, and head over to the Colonels office. The sun was already up, and the humidity was rising. This was not like D.C., even with it's famous humidity, nor, certainly was it like Milwaukee.

I met Chuck down the Hall. He had been up since 0400, and had already had a cup of coffee. He had one waiting for me, but it had gotten cold. I drank it anyway. He filled me in a bit more on the prospective route we would be taking. He assured me that although there might be a few hostiles, that it would be, for the most part, pretty safe, at least until we got close to the Cambodian border end of the tunnels. We would try to meet up with the Montagnards about 10 klicks from where our mission would become hairy.

We picked up Paul in front of the enlisted barracks. He was drinking a cup of hot coffee. I wanted to grab it from him. I needed a hot cup of coffee. They both assured me that Colonel Frey would have a large pot of coffee in his office. We reached the office and parked the jeep directly in front. The Marine guards recognized us from the day before and saluted and waved us in.

Colonel Frey was already sitting at his desk, reviewing maps, and intelligence reports from the night before.

"Come in gentlemen, we have a number of things to go over before you take off on your trek this morning. First of all, have a cup of coffee. The coffee pot is over there on the other desk, and the cups are in the drawer. Help yourselves."

We each poured ourselves a cup of coffee. There is nothing like a cup of Navy, and in this case Marine Corps coffee. Strong. A spoon can almost stand up in it. We sat down without being asked. Formality before a mission was not a priority. Some military protocol, however, always is.

"Chuck, you are in charge of this mission, as we have already discussed. That means you will have tactical leadership, as well as operational leadership. If you say it is a go, then it is a go. If you say abort, then the mission will be aborted. There will be no communication with base, and that means me. Basically you will be on your own. The three of you are experts in your fields, and with a bit of luck, no, a lot of luck, the mission can be a success. Granted, it is unorthodox. Unorthodox, but absolutely necessary. And, there is one more thing. This is completely top secret, and you can never talk about it when you get back. And, it would be best if you never talked about it, even when you get back to 'the world.' Clearly you know why. LSD, marijuana, can you believe we are using those things in war? Just know that I was not the one who dreamed this up. It actually came from up top. I am not at liberty to say how up top, but suffice it to say, above my pay grade. So basically you will get to General Diem, capture him and get him to reveal whatever impending offensive they are planning. We are pretty certain that there is something impending. Clearly you cannot just release him after you get the information, so you will have to do what you have to do. Am I clear?"

When I heard that, I was about to say that there was no way I could take part in executing someone, when Chuck spoke up and said, "We will take care of everything as indicated, sir."

"In that case, Chuck, Tom, Paul, dismissed. We are counting on you. God speed, and for God's sake, don't get caught."

The three of us said, "Yes sir," but before we left, Chuck took the medical box.

All I could think about was, "Don't get caught." FUBAR!

CHAPTER 20

West Toward The Tunnels and The Cambodian Border

L eaving the base, and passing Tan Son Nhut airfield, I felt that I was leaving civilization. The road we were taking was between the Saigon River and the Vam Co Dong River, not a very good road, and not even remotely like Highway One, which was no great shakes either, but this road took us west in the direction of Ben Dinh and Tran Bang. Ben Dinh is approximately fifty kilometers from Saigon, and was known to have an elaborate tunnels system, and was near the western end of the known Cu Chi tunnels. This area, according to intelligence reports, was where General Diem and his staff were holed up. Much of the area had been doused with Agent Orange, and had also been napalmed, so it was pretty much defoliated, making it much more difficult to either hide, or approach, without anyone seeing you. As we approached the turn off to Ben Dinh, Chuck veered left in a fork in the road. We were now headed toward Trang Bang, which was even closer to Cambodia. I asked if we were, in fact, going to go into Cambodia. I wanted to go there less than I wanted to stay in Viet Nam. I had heard about all the bad things that happened there, even to the native Cambodians. Chuck assured me that we were not going into Cambodia, and that our target area was not much farther, but that soon we would have to park and hide the jeep and hump in on foot. The three of us were in pretty good shape, and the medical box was not all that heavy. We would take turns carrying it, while the other two would be have rifles at the ready. I thought about protesting that I was a non-combatant, and therefore was not supposed to be carrying a rifle, but that protest would have been to no avail. And, quite frankly I was not that naive. I felt much more secure, however, with my knife in its sheath, on my belt. It was a ten inch serrated blade, and could serve a multitude of purposes. As a weapon, I felt much more comfortable in handling the knife than the rifle. Maybe because when and where I grew up, carrying a knife was not all that unusual. Maybe because I really hadn't fired a rifle before, other than, perhaps, at the arcade I took Carolyn to in Milwaukee, where I won her a bear. But then I was not using real bullets. Hopefully I would not be faced with using a real rifle as a weapon. I was not certain I could ever kill anyone, even in self- defense. I suspect that most of the young men here in the Nam felt that way before they went to boot camp, or even after. And I had not gone to boot camp. I was banking on Chuck getting us through the mission without any need to use a weapon. I wasn't sure how Paul felt about that. I assumed that inasmuch as he was a corpsman, the need to save, rather than take a life, was his orientation. Yet, he did seem pretty confident about basic humping in the field, giving me the impression that there as more to this corpsman than met the eye. The thought that he and Chuck seemed to have served together in the past, started to creep into my mind.

We had driven for what seemed like the entire day, but in actuality it was only four hours. The Sun although still high, was a bit lower on the horizon. We kept driving. The road was full of potholes, probably caused by the bombing and the chemicals and napalm which no doubt hit most of everything. The entire tunnel area had been strafed at one time or another, and usually frequently. I hoped our side knew we were on the road, so they wouldn't douse us with that defoliant that came in a large can with an orange stripe on it, or hit us with napalm. I kept thinking about the little girl on the Repose who was burned by the napalm. A casualty of war. I hated it.

Pauly was the first to see them. The Montagnards were off to the port side of the jeep, about one klick away. He told Chuck, who then saw them and waved and turned in their direction. We were now off the road and in knee-deep grass. The jeep held up to its reputation and held its own against the tall grass. We approached the Montagnards, and the tribal leader approached the jeep. He and Chuck conversed. Was Chuck fluent in Montagnard too? Unbelievable! It turns out that they actually really spoke in French. The French was sort of a patois, but not the kind they speak in New Orleans, but rather a mixture of French, Vietnamese and English. I could understand some of it, but the cadence threw me off. Also, I was distracted by the number of Montagnards hiding in the bushes. Bushes that grow back after defoliation, sturdier and heavier. But, from what I could hear, I thought I heard Ben Duoc several times.

That was confirmed when Chuck turned to Paul and me and said, "We are going to Ben Duoc. The chief here says he has spotted who he believes is General Diem. Apparently General Diem, and the same aide d'camp, leave the tunnel around the same time, each day, and the General smokes a cigar. I wonder if it's Cuban. He says that they are always alone for at least an hour, and then either return to the tunnel or several of his men come out and then they return to the tunnel. That might be our way to snatch him, and his trusty side kick, who might know just about as much as does the General. So, ladies, we will snatch them both, and we might not even have to use the LSD and pot on him, and maybe not even his platoon or company or whatever is down there with him. This is looking like it might be easier than I thought."

Nothing sounded easy from my point of view.

The three of us got out of the jeep, grabbed our gear, including the medical box, and followed the Montagnard chief. The chief turned and came over to me and shook my hand, and then went to Paul and shook his as well, but with both hands. It was almost like

BAC SI

he knew Paul too. I knew Chuck had been out in the bush, but I didn't program in that Pauly had any humping experience. But, he was a corpsman, so why wouldn't he have had some time out in the bush? I guess I was the only rookie. Maybe I was a rookie out here, but I wasn't clueless in battle. The difference was, however, that the battles I fought were in Gary, and usually on a one to one basis, or two to one at most, not with an enemy of anywhere between ten and fifty guys who were sworn to kill you.

I did carry one of the rifles, but had it slung rather than at the ready, much to Chuck's chagrin. I did keep one hand on my knife. Anytime there was movement in the bush I started to unsheathe my knife, as if that would do anything against an AK-47, the Russian, and later the Chinese made rifle used by the VC.

It was getting dark, yet not dark enough to break out flashlights. As if using flashlights would have been the smart thing to do. And besides, the Montagnards knew this area like the back of their hands. We followed in their footsteps, not only because of the increasingly poor visibility due to the developing darkness, but also because of the potential booby traps. There were pits around the tunnels. In these pits there were often the notorious punji sticks, the sharpened bamboo stalks usually smeared with feces. If you were unlucky enough to step on a leaf covered pit, and you fell into one of these pits, you would be out for the count, even if it were "only" a foot puncture. There were stories of having to have one's foot or leg amputated because of the infection resulting from a punji stick booby trap. Other pits were filled with kraits, the highly venomous snake, indigenous to Viet Nam. No one survived the pits filled with the kraits. So, we were careful and deliberate, and actually followed in the direct footsteps of our host guides. The Montagnards could almost see in the dark. Of course they also knew this area because it was their homeland, and it had been for centuries. On top of that, they came to hate the North Viet Nam Army, and the VC were a close second.

Yet, there was no way they could fight the North Vietnamese. So, they aided "The enemy of their enemy."

They led us to a clearing that was surrounded by trees that had not been defoliated. The pointed to the middle of a vast defoliated area and pointed out some change in topography, namely dirt, grass and tree branches that were out of place. That area was the covering for the tunnels. We looked through our binoculars and saw that, in fact, the ground had been disturbed, and yes the covering did look a bit artificially arranged. It looked like the Montagnards were right. This apparently was the opening to the tunnel system in this area. Chuck then asked the chief where the water supply for the tunnels was, not really knowing if the chief would know that. Apparently there were two water supplies. One was water brought in by way of drums from the north, along the Ho Chi Minh trail, and the second came from water gallons filled at the Saigon River, not too far away. This water had to be purified, by means of purification tablets or by boiling. After the chief pointed this out, there was nothing much else the Montagnards could do, so Chuck thanked them, shook hands with the chief, and bid them adieu. Before he left, the chief came over and shook Pauly's hand and then mine.

He thanked me and called me by my name, "Bac Si." He knew.

As the chief and his men left, I had an empty feeling. There is a certain security in numbers, even if the number only had knives, spears, and bows and arrows. We took cover in the trees and waited. We didn't know how long we would have to wait. Maybe the General wouldn't be taking his usual cigar break. Maybe he was no longer there. Maybe they had already struck and were either ensconced back in the vast tunnel system, or they had fled north to rejoin a battalion. Darkness is the bush can be a bit intimidating. Strange sounds and movements are everywhere. For a city guy, even from Gary, Indiana, the smallest noise can be disturbing. It was that way all evening and throughout the night. And, still no sign of our target. The Sun came up and so did the temperature. We did have our canteens with us, and had some dried food with us. We were careful not to bring anything that gave off an odor. You never knew how much a scent could travel and be picked up. Animals have a keen sense of smell, so why couldn't humans, and especially one's enemy. So we munched on Hershey Bars, and that certainly kept our sugar levels up. We took turns sleeping, three hours at a time. No movement from the area suspected as being the entrance to the tunnel. Night fell again, and it was dark because this night, clouds covered the moon, so it was pitch black. It was then we saw an opening of the tunnel. It was slight at first, barely noticeable, but the ground around some leaves and tree limbs began to shift. Then a barely perceptible light, a pin light. But that was all it took. We focused our binoculars on the pin light, and then we saw the ground open up, like a trap door. It was in fact a trap door. The ground, leaves and limbs were securely fastened to the trap door, so what we saw was not dirt moving, but the entire door moving. They had secured it so well, that were it not for the pin light, we would never have seen it. Slowly the trap door opened more widely and a head appeared. The head was wearing the helmet of the North Vietnamese Army. The head deliberately looked around, making a virtual 360-degree scan of the terrain. The head made another sweep, and then disappeared back into the tunnel. We kept quiet and hoped that the head was signaling someone else that the coast was clear. We were right. Approximately two minutes later, the head appeared, and then his shoulders and finally the rest of him. Once he was completely out of the tunnel, he again scanned the area. After another deliberate scrutiny of the area, he held the trap door open, and out emerged another person, but this one was not wearing a helmet. He was wearing a campaign hat of an officer in the NVA. He wore braiding on his right shoulder, and a pistol on his right hip. He too looked around and surveyed the area. Through my binoculars I saw his face, at least in profile. He had the same profile features of the Vietnamese official, Mr. Diem, who was a patient aboard the Repose.

Or, was my mind playing tricks on me. After all, the expression that "they all look alike," isn't necessarily pejorative. To people of different races, facial characteristics often seem similar. But I could swear that this man was the spitting image of the patient who spoke with me and told me about a possibly impending assault. Of course, why wouldn't they resemble one another, they were brothers.

I scanned the first man who came out of the tunnel, and he too looked vaguely familiar. He was much younger than the man for whom he held the trap door open. The officer took out a cigar and wet it with his saliva, bit off the end and placed the cigar in his mouth. The young soldier dutifully struck a match and lit it for his superior officer.

I overheard the officer say, "Cam on." (Thank you). They took in the night air for a moment and then began to walk. All the while, the young soldier scanned the area, unslung his AK-47, and kept his rifle at the ready. Clearly this young man was dedicated to protect the officer. The three of us kept silent and almost perfectly still. Any slight noise or movement might give us away. If that happened, either the young soldier could shoot us, the two of them could duck back into the tunnel, or the soldiers who were no doubt down in the tunnel would stream out like ants out of an ant hill and come after us. And, of course, whichever of those things occurred, the mission would be blown, and any planned enemy assault could take place without us being able to warn anyone, not to mention whatever might happen to us. So, we kept still, and watched.

We didn't move and we apparently could read each other's minds, that we would do nothing right now. After the officer finished his cigar, he and the young soldier returned to the tunnel trap door entrance, and descended. Chuck, Pauly and I breathed a sigh of relief and then moved farther back into the tree line. We then talked and agreed that it was best if we waited until the next night to make our move. We spent the entire next day watching the tunnel entrance, hoping that there were not multiple openings too close by. Certainly there were more egresses to the tunnel, but more than likely they would not be too close together. At least that is what we hoped. So, we waited. The day dragged on, as did the heat. A diet of Hershey Bars and water didn't exactly help the situation. The sugar also made us a bit hyper. Finally, night fell again, and once again we lucked out. The moon was covered by clouds, as it was the night before, so once again the night was pitch black. At about the same time as the previous night, there was a slight movement of the ground, leaves and limbs around the tunnel entrance. The pin light showed again, and the trap door lifted. The same soldier, as far as we could tell, slowly lifted out of the tunnel, held the trap door open for the same officer, and out they came and began their walk about, with the officer smoking his nightly cigar. We knew we had to strike. This time Chuck and Pauly donned leaf and straw camouflage and were on the ground. They both had their knives drawn. They clearly could not risk taking a shot, because the noise would alert whoever was down in the tunnel. I remained in the tree line, watching. I would alert them if anyone else was around or coming toward them. The NVA used a whistle to signal an attack. I, too, would use a whistle if Chuck and Paul were about to be discovered. In that way, the soldiers down in the tunnel might think that it was another NVA platoon attacking a U.S. position. At least that is what we decided. The officer and the soldier were walking a bit farther from the tunnel entrance than they had the night before. They were walking parallel to where Chuck and Paul were hiding in the camouflage clumps of grass and leaves. The camouflage, made by the Montagnards, blended in perfectly. Clearly the prey didn't detect its stalker. I watched as Chuck and Paul inched closer to the two Vietnamese. They were so stealth that I wondered how and where they had learned that. Then they pounced. Chuck grabbed the officer and with his hand around the officer's mouth and the knife held at his throat, he turned the officer's head. He spoke softly into his ear, in Vietnamese, saying that he would snap his neck if he made a sound. Paul did the same to the soldier.

The words I could make out were "Ca Ca Dau," which meant, "I'll kill you."

I had never heard those words in anger before. Both the officer and soldier, no doubt, knew that Chuck and Pauly were serious. They offered no resistance. So Chuck and Paul moved their quarry into the tree line, where I met them.

CHAPTER 21

The Interrogation

I quickly placed duct tape over the mouths of both the officer and the soldier, while Chuck and Paul tied their hands behind their backs and secured their hand ropes to their ankles. Quite simply they were hog-tied. We felt that we would only have less than a half an hour to decide what we were going to do with them, or to them. Try to get them to talk now, and quickly? Try to get them back to the jeep and get back to Saigon? Try to blow up the tunnel to prevent the ants from coming out of the hill when they realized that their officer had not returned from his nightly cigar? What in the hell were we going to do with the LSD and pot? We could still have time to put the LSD into their water supply if we could find it, and if the water was stored above ground and not in the tunnel. Although we had thought out much of the plan, we clearly didn't think it completely through, so we were going to have to improvise. Actually Chuck knew what he was doing, and what would or should happen next. Pauly was getting a bit anxious with the captured young soldier. The soldier looked young, very young. My guess was that the kid was about 15 or 16 years old, but of course many Vietnamese look young, especially to occidentals. The kid had fear in his eyes, but the officer did not. I approached the young man and spoke to him in Vietnamese. I told him that we did not want to hurt him, and that all we wanted was some information. I told him that we knew he was only doing his job, and that although he believed that his side was right, and that I knew that the North Vietnamese government wanted the Americans out of their land, that we were only there because the people of the South asked us to be there and help them keep their own way of life. I told him that I knew many Vietnamese people and that I was a "Bac Si," and had helped many of his people. I went on to tell him that one of my first patients was a little girl just a little younger than he, who was from South Viet Nam, and who had to flee because of the fighting, and that she had a brother who also had to flee, but he went north, even though he hated what the North was doing to the country. He looked at me with eyes that were watering rather than angry. But, who could really tell? My diagnostic skills out here in the bush might be affected by fear, my own.

The young soldier reluctantly told me his name, Tran, but would say no more. I thought,"Tran? I knew that name, but from where?" I dismissed it, thinking that Tran is a fairly common name in Viet Nam. His eyes kept darting back to his superior officer. Chuck got the officer to give his rank and his name. General Diem of the People's Army of Viet Nam. So this was, in fact, the General Diem we were hoping to find. Like the young soldier, he would offer no more information. We had little time, so we had to make a decision about what to do next. We were, at least in theory, committed to trying to get the LSD into the water supply of the troops in the tunnel. That way we could spirit away the General so that Command could extract whatever information they could from him. We also knew that we might also have to get some of the drugs into General Diem and possibly his aide, Tran.

Paul came up with the first suggestion, and within earshot of both General Diem and Tran. "Maybe we should kill them now and get the LSD into their troops and then grab a couple of them and get whatever information we can from them, and then waste however many we can."

Chuck didn't say a word, but I almost screamed, "Absolutely not! We aren't killing anyone, capice?" I reverted back to my Italian roots.

Paul then said, "Well OK Bac Si, you are the interrogation genius here. You tell us what we should do next. We need to get information from these gooks, and we need to get it nhanh nyaang (fast)." Paul was getting more and more edgy. Clearly he was out of his element, in spite of having been in the bush many times.

I said, "Ok Pauly, let's all calm down and think this through. We do have a bit of time, at least a cigar length of time."

I walked over to General Diem, and told him outright, "General Diem, I spoke with your brother on the Hospital Ship Repose. He told me that you got him a message warning him that something was going to happen soon, and for him to get out of Saigon, which he did. He was injured when a bomb blew up a G.I. bar in downtown Saigon. Why he would have been there we haven't quite figured out, but he was. He did have a head injury, and it was first thought to be fairly severe. Since he was a prominent South Viet Nam official, he was taken to the Repose, rather than treated locally. I think now that somehow he en-gineered being sent to the Navy ship. Now we need information from you about the impending assault or operation. I can tell you, if any of our Marines are killed as a result of this operation, you will die, as will your brother, and as will your entire family. We will track down every member of your family and make them pay for every Marine death resulting from you not telling us what we need to know. And, we will use drugs on you, and make you into a crazy man, before we kill you, and we will do the same to your family, hieu hee.oo (understand)?"

Chuck was surprised at my tactic. So was I. I did sound convincing though, and that was my plan. I didn't want to kill anyone. Get them a bit high, well I could tolerate that, but kill someone? No way. That was simply not in my DNA. The General looked at me, at first unbe-lieving, but then I saw something in his eyes. Fear. I then continued in Vietnamese, telling him that I knew that he must have wanted to not only save his brother from whatever would be coming, but I couldn't help but feel that he knew that his brother would tell the Americans.

After all, the Americans and the South Vietnamese were allies.

Tran clearly overheard what the General was saying. He looked startled. He tried to murmur something but the duct tape prevented him from opening his mouth to speak. Pauly wasn't about to take off the duct tape for fear of Tran yelling out to warn his compatriots in the tunnel. I spoke to Tran, although I was standing in front of the General.

"Tran, we do not want to hurt you, and if you and the General cooperate with us and give us the information we need to protect our troops from any impending offensive, we will make certain that you will not be harmed, by either side, hieu hee.oo (understand)?"

He nodded, still with fear in his eyes. It was then, again, I could see how young he was. This was a mere boy.

The General indicated that he wanted to speak, and we took a chance and loosened the duct tape so he could speak a bit, but yet not yell.

He spoke softly, and said, "Leave the boy alone. He is innocent and is only doing what he has been ordered to do. If you have any decency you will spare him. I am the one you want, and I am the one who has the information you seek."

Tran shook his head vigorously from side to side, clearly not wanting his superior officer to shield him. Still, the fear in his eyes betrayed him. He was a boy in the presence of a father figure. That was obvious, the night before, in the way he lit the General's cigar. And, clearly the General had paternal feelings about the boy.

Time was ticking, and we had to do something. Do we just abscond with the General and his aide? Do we drug them? Do we drug whoever is in the tunnel, and if so, how? There was no right choice here, just a bunch of possibilities, all of which had repercussions, some good and some not so good. I was not a warrior and therefore tactical moves on a battlefield were above my pay grade, or maybe below my pay grade. My only job on this mission was to extract the needed information from the General, ostensibly using mind-altering drugs. But, it was becoming more apparent that maybe we might have to use the LSD to get the information. Yet, we might have to use it to sedate the troops.

While I was talking with the General, Chuck was out doing some reconnaissance. He had left the General in my custody, securely tied of course. He had actually tied him to a tree.

When he returned he said, "I located the water cans. I think these are major water supplies. One of them has a hose leading from it and disappearing into the ground. My guess is that it is feeding right into the tunnel, and that the gooks are using it primarily for their drinking water." He whispered into my ear, "See if you can get the General to reveal if that is where they are drinking from. How hot is it down there. It has to be stifling, even if they have fans for air circulation and ventilation. If it is as hot as I can only imagine it is down there then they must be drinking a lot of water, so they won't dehydrate."

Instead of going immediately after the General, I walked back over to Tran. I told him to nod yes or no to the questions I would ask him. First I asked him how many people were down in the tunnel in this area, 30? He nodded no. I asked, 20? He nodded no once again. I asked "More than 30?" He nodded no. I asked him "Less than 10?" and he nodded yes. "Five?" He nodded yes. Now, could we believe him? Certainly closer to Saigon there must be many more. But we were more concerned about how many in this immediate area, the one's with the General. In many ways it didn't matter. If we put all of the LSD into the water, all of the VC or NVA in the area that relied on this particular water supply would all be seeing bright lights, stars, colors and visions anyway. But, it would be useful to know how many would come out eventually. But, of course, we would be long gone. If their trip lasted for 12 hours or more, and if we cold get the information we needed, then we would be home free. We would relay the intel back to Colonel Frey, at the Command Center, and the mission would be accomplished, and troops being saved, at least from any immediate planned offensive. So, it appeared that that part of the decision was made. Put the drugs into the water supply. We did need to keep some of the acid, so we could extract information from General Diem and Tran, if necessary. And then of course, we had the pot.

Chuck crawled over to the tube which lead from one of the water vats, which was really a large can, the size of an oil drum. As a matter of fact, that is what it was, an oil drum. He took out a hypodermic needle and loaded the cartridge with LSD, and injected it into the tubing leading underground. He then loaded the cartridge again. He did that a total of 20 times. If that amount of LSD didn't create a hallucinatory state for everyone from the Cambodian border to Saigon, I would be in awe, and would put them up against an entire city of our most hardcore druggies back in the States. San Francisco came to mind, from what I heard. Now the question would be how long would it take for the residents of the tunnel to get high enough so they either wouldn't notice that their general wasn't there, or wouldn't care. Either way, we would be long gone, and either back at Command or close enough to communicate at least a preliminary warning alert of what might be coming down. The General saw what Chuck was doing, and began to struggle against his bonds. Tran was more docile, yet kept his eyes on what was happening to the General. Paul was making certain that the General's hands were still securely tied and that the rope that held him virtually tethered to the tree was still holding as it was supposed to.

Paul then smiled and said to the General, "You're next General, unless you give us the information we want. We want you to tell us about the planned operation that your warned your brother about. My guess is that Tran here also knows about what is planned, am I right?"

The General remained stoic and also stopped struggling. Paul took a syringe and plunged it into a vial of the fluid containing a concentration of LSD, and cleared the air bubbles out of the syringe and needle.

The General's eyes widened and he spoke in English. "You can't do that to me. That is against the Geneva Convention."

Paul fired back and said, "Tell that to our guys you are holding in the Hanoi Hilton."

I left Tran's side and went to Paul and said, "Pauly, you can't do that. It's not right. We have to give him a chance to cooperate. And besides, he's an old man. You don't know the dosage, and what he can tolerate. You might put him in cardiac arrest. You don't want to kill him. You just can't kill him. I won't let you kill him."

Pauly calmed down, but I could see that he was pissed. I knew that he wasn't pissed at the General, but what he represented. And, no doubt, being a corpsman to companies of Marines, in the field, I know he saw more than his share of death and trauma as a result of his enemy, and General Diem was his enemy. Inevitably, war does that to man.

I told Pauly that if anyone was going to handle the interrogation of General Diem, and inject him if necessary, it would be me. The interrogation part of this mission was my responsibility. Granted, I wasn't thrilled about the usage of LSD in interrogations, sanctioned Army experiments not withstanding, and as a psychologist I was not an injector, although I did know how. But this was war, albeit still referred to as a "conflict." I had another idea. Tran seemed to me as being vulnerable. He was young, and therefore didn't have the ingrained defense mechanisms as well as the experience to resist manipulation like the General would have with his experience and age. So I whispered to Paul, and when Chuck returned from "turning on" the troops in the tunnel, I whispered to him as well, that I was going to take Tran back into the tree line and interrogate him, without using drugs, but rather with logic, motivational manipulation, and persuasion. That is, if I could. But, I had to give it a go, and again, I reminded Chuck and Paul that that was my job to do, and not theirs. Their job was more tactical, and although with Pauly, to some extent medical, but mine was interrogation through mind control, using sound psychological principles of course. Yeah sure!

I unloosened Tran from the tree, although keeping his hands bound with a rope connecting his bound hands to the ropes binding his feet. The restraints on his feet allowed him to shuffle walk with very short steps, but if he tried to run he would trip and have difficulty getting back on his feet without assistance. I kept the duct tape on over his mouth. He could breathe and murmur, but that is about all.

As I walked Tran deeper into the tree line, I looked back and saw General Diem watching. His eyes conveyed deep concern. Was it concern for the young man who was being led to who knows where for who knows what, or was it because he had figured out that the young man was going to be interrogated? He had to be wondering and concerned about the young soldier's ability to resist giving information under the stress of interrogation. And, I was sure he was worried that I would be using LSD on Tran to extract the information.

Still, time was of the essence.

I led Tran to a slight clearing approximately 30 yards from where Chuck and Paul were keeping watch on General Diem, and the entrance to the tunnel. I told him to sit on the ground and lean against a tree. He actually had to kneel and had to sit back on his haunches. But, he quickly relaxed a bit. His eyes never left me and it was clear that he was still frightened. Frightened but angry. I spoke to him in Vietnamese. I asked him where he was from in Viet Nam. I asked him if he had family. I asked him how old he was. I asked him if he really hated the Americans. He glared at me. He still couldn't talk because of the duct tape. I wasn't sure if I could or should remove the tape from his mouth. I knew for certain that I could not remove the bindings on his hands and feet. His hand restraints kept his hands behind his back, but his hands rested on his feet. Leaning against the tree gave him some slack. He was actually wearing boots rather than the Ho Chi Minh sandals that the majority of the VC wore. This was probably because he was an aide to a general.

When Chuck had searched the general and Tran, he took from them the pocket booklets they usually carried, much like our dog tags. Usually in their identification booklets there was something personal like a picture of a girlfriend, wife, or family. Americans being the sentimental slobs that they are, more often than not, kept the identification but put the picture back into the pocket of the captive. That certainly wasn't true when the VC or NVA captured an American. I hadn't thought about that much, and didn't think I needed to go back and get the identification booklet to see if I could glean anything from it, and use it in my interrogation. I thought I would just have to rely on my training and knowledge of stress and motivation to extract information from this young man.

I sat on the ground directly in front of him and said, "Tran, I know you are just doing your job, and I know you love your country. I love your country too. That is why I am here, to help your country. Your country asked me, us, to come here. My country believes in many freedoms, including freedom to choose the kind of government you want. If the people of your country want to choose a democracy, we are here to help them get that. If the majority of people choose to have a communist form of government, we might not like it, but so be it. But you know as well as I that at least half of the people in your country want a democratic form of government, even if there is some corruption in it. You can't tell me that in the communist North that there isn't corruption there as well. You are young. Our young people in America also have issues with our government, but they can chose, and they can change the people who govern by a simply vote. You as a young person surely has to want a vote, a say in how you live, don't you? Why I am here with you right now is that many innocent people, most of them young, probably your age, will die. We know that there is something planned to attack some of our troops. If that happens, many, many young men will die, both on our side as well as yours.

You and I might not be able to end this war, but we can save innocent young men, young men your age. I don't know you Tran, but I don't want you to die, and I think that down deep you don't want me to die. Can't you and I get together just this one time and save innocent boys? Just this once? Maybe if we do this together this once, maybe it will catch on and the fighting will end sooner, and the war will end. You and I will have done our jobs and we, you and I, will have saved lives, Vietnamese as well as American. I have been deeply touched by your people, Tran. I treated a little girl from Viet Nam, last year, and she lost her family because of this war. Her mother and father were killed, in her village, and her brother had to flee so he wouldn't be killed. She saw her home burned down, and she is now without a mother, father, brother and her home. I know you have seen much fighting in this war, but please Tran, just for a minute, try to put yourself in that little girl's place. She was young, just like you. Can we please save some young lives? Can we not have at least a few lives not changed so tragically like that little girl?"

At first Tran looked startled, like someone had told him something important to him that he thought no one else knew. He then looked at me and nodded. I read him to be sincere in his response. I then asked him if I could take off the duct tape without him yelling out. He nodded again in the affirmative. I looked into his eyes, and again I read him as being sincere. I could almost detect a tear in his eyes, but that might have been my wishful thinking.

So, I took a chance and removed the duct tape. And, true to his affirmative nod, he did not scream. Rather, he said, "Cam on, Bac Si" (Thank you doctor).

We exchanged a couple of pleasantries, if you can ever exchange pleasantries with an enemy at war. But I asked him where he was from, and if he had family. He told me that he was from the South, and that he did have a family, but no more. I didn't want to push it with the family questioning since there was a good chance that his family was killed by Americans, either directly or indirectly. So, again, I began my appeal about saving lives of young men his age, on both sides. I told him that I understood revolution, and that my country had its beginning by revolution. I shared with him a personal note, that I really did not want to be here, and that I knew that many of our soldiers didn't want to be here either. I even showed him my "love beads," and explained to him what they were. He smiled a bit. I asked him if he would like them, and if he did that I would give them to him. He nodded in the affirmative. I unclasped the beads from around my neck and placed them around his.

He smiled again and once again said "Cam on, Bac Si."

As I finished putting my cherished love beads, my bit of rebellion against the system, around his neck, he was still essentially kneeling on his haunches, with his hands still tied and then tied again to his ankles and feet. I really should not have been so trusting. All of the sudden, he came at me with a knife. It was smaller than my ten inch serrated blade but a knife nevertheless. When he was searched, his shoes were not removed. Apparently he had a knife concealed in his shoe. When he sat back on his haunches, he was able to reach his shoe and the concealed knife, cut the ropes off of his hands, as well as the one binding his hands to his feet, as he was hog tied.

He came at me so suddenly and said "Ca Ca Dau, Bac si" (I'll kill you, Bac si).

He thrust his knife into my chest, but I moved back in time to thwart the full impact, and the knife penetrated only about an inch into me. Reflexively I had my knife out and thrust it up from the sheath at my waist, and into his gut. As he was moving forward to stab me, coupled with my counter thrust forward and up, my ten-inch blade went all the way into him. Hs eyes widened and started to scream, but I covered his mouth with my left hand and my right hand held the knife into him. He slumped, but I held him in that position for what seemed like eternity, but was actually probably only a minute or so, and he shuttered and died. That young boy died in my arms.

"Oh Jesus forgive me." I kept whispering, "Oh Jesus forgive me. Oh Jesus forgive me. Oh Jesus forgive me." I killed another human being. I killed a little boy. It didn't matter that he was going to kill me. I killed a little boy. "Oh Jesus forgive me."

I was bleeding, but Tran's knife had not hit either my heart or my lung. I knew I would live, but I was bleeding profusely. I had laid Tran down by the tree, and actually retied his hands and reapplied the duct tape to his mouth, for whatever good that might have been, and staggered back out of the deep part of the tree line and found Chuck and Paul, with General Diem. They looked at me and clearly knew something happened. The saw me bleeding, and clearly I did not have Tran with me. Would I have been so stupid as to leave him unattended? Had he escaped? Was I able to get any information from him? Why was I bleeding?

Chuck spoke first. "What in the hell happened Tommy? Where is Tran? Did you get him to talk?"

I fell to the ground and Pauly ran over to me and saw the blood. He tore open my shirt and immediately started treating me, as all good corpsmen would do. I had lost a lot of blood and was going into shock. They had to get me out of there, but the mission had to be completed. More than just my life was at stake here. Pauly put me on the ground and tried to stop the bleeding with pressure. He told me to continue putting pressure on the wound and quickly got his medical kit, opened it and found the antiseptic powder and shook it on my wound. He then sutured it up and immediately the bleeding stopped. He gave me some morphine for the pain. I guess I am stronger than I thought. I started to sit up. I guess the adrenaline was kicking in. I asked for some water. I took a few sips and felt a bit better. The guilt I was feeling was intense. I kept thinking that I killed a man, I killed a boy. I knew that that nothing could ever expiate my guilt. I began to weep.

I began beating my breast, "Mea culpa, mea culpa, mea maxima culpa."

Chuck slapped me across the face and said, "Tommy, you have to snap out of any guilt trip you might be on. There is something that we still have to do. Something that you have to do. It is more important than what you were forced to do. You did not kill a man, you fought for your life and the lives of others, and that man, that boy, died. You have to remind yourself of that now, and always. You did not kill someone, you were being attacked and you had to protect yourself and us. Tran could have just as easily killed you, snuck up on us and killed us, and then freed General Diem and warned his troops and then the offensive that was planned would go on unchallenged, with many, many of our Marines, surprised and killed."

I knew I would live, and I also knew I had something else to do. Chuck was right, and his words sunk in. They didn't necessarily absolve me of my guilt, but putting the killing of Tran into perspective and shaking me into my duty, went a long way. It got me to go on. I would have to interrogate the General. Chuck and Pauly might be too angry not to do something foolish. As I sat there, the General was watching all of this. He called out and asked what had happened to his soldier. He wasn't concerned about me at all. He was the enemy, and we had to remember that. I had Pauly take me over to the General. I told him what had happened to Tran. He was quiet for a moment or so, and then smiled and said "Then he died a hero."

I said, "No General, he died, and it was a waste, and it is all your fault. You now are going to tell me what we need to know or the injection of the drug you get will be of something lethal."

But then, almost as I finished my threat, which there was no way I would carry out, nor allow my compatriots to carry out either, the General began to sing, and then began to rotate his head and smile and laugh and speak in a combination of Vietnamese and French. Clearly he was starting to "trip out." Chuck and Pauly decided while I was with

Tran, to go ahead and inject the LSD intravenously into the General. Usually LSD is ingested with food or drink, or even just absorbed through the skin, but the much faster way, although more dangerous, is intravenous injection. It is much, much quicker. Although this is not what I would have allowed, it had already been injected and we were getting short on time, so I didn't make an issue of it. And, as it could turn out, this was good, from a possible interrogation point of view, or at least that is what I rationalized, and secretly hoped.

I hoped I could re-direct him from the hallucinations, the psychedelic lights and any voices he might be hearing. Chuck and Paul were keeping their eyes on the area of the entrance to the tunnel. It was now just a matter of time. The General and Tran had been gone approximately an hour. The night before, the cigar session lasted only about forty-five minutes. It is mind-boggling how much had transpired in only less than an hour. Hopefully, the troops underground were thirsty enough to drink enough of the water laced with LSD, so that they too would be experiencing those beautiful colors, all the while not caring about the war, the enemy, or anything else for that matter. I knelt next to the General and put my hand on his shoulder. I spoke only Vietnamese to him. I began to tell him that he was courageous and had led his troops and directed others to a decisive assault on the Americans. I told him that his brother was safe and secure, and although he had been injured in a blast last week, that he was recuperating on the American's hospital ship, and was therefore safe from the recent offensive. I then told him that as a result of his heroic assault on the Americans that he was being awarded the highest honor in the Army of North Viet Nam. Hanoi only needed to have the particulars, as only he knew them, so they could write it on the proclamations to be published and posted on all of the government buildings in Hanoi. He would be awarded the medal when he returned to the Capital. He smiled as he continued tripping and moving his head from side to side, clearly enjoying the sights.

CHAPTER 22

The Information

The General was on the acid trip of a lifetime. The intravenous injection not only worked quickly, but also intensely. The amount was not exactly measured. He could have just as easily stroked out or have had a heart attack. He clearly was in good shape, and his body was able to absorb the drug much like "a hippie" might. So, I kept up with the compliments on his offensive. I appealed to his military vanity, which I only assumed he had. I was right. The information began to flow. But, at the same time, the "ants, in fact, came out of the ant hill." The ground covered entrance to the tunnel opened. Not slowly and deliberate, as one would expect, but rather loudly and not at all subtle. The first ones out were singing and weaving, barely able to climb out of the tunnel on their own. As a matter of fact, the first few had to be almost pushed out of the tunnel by their cohorts, who were also singing and clearly tripping. It was almost comical to watch if we weren't in a battle for our lives and the lives of many of our men. Chuck and Pauly had their rifles at the ready, still not trusting the lasting effects of the LSD on those soldiers. Those soldiers also looked young. Some of them looked even younger than Tran. Some of them probably were his age. But, some of our soldiers and Marines are that young too, I thought. God, war is hell. Some of the enemy were waving their rifles or pistols in the air, in an almost bravado way. The LSD was clearly breaking down inhibitions. And, this is what I was hoping that it was doing to General Diem, in spite of my initial misgivings to using the drug.

I again complimented General Diem for his cunning and his excellent planning of offensive, especially for the upcoming one. He smiled and said that yes, it was a brilliantly conceived plan and that there would be one hundred and fifty young patriots raining down on the enemy. I again reiterated that Hanoi was so very proud of him, he went on to say that his men would soon be out of the tunnels and swarming all over the base, and that the entire airfield would be immobilized for months.

I said, "Tan Son Nhut?"

He laughed and said "Of course. Isn't it beautiful, just like all the colors."

We had the information. Hopefully it was accurate, and the intel we needed. But, could we rely on the efficacy of the drug. Dr. Van Murray Sim, who had conducted the LSD experiments, and who was the founder of the Edgewood Arsenal's Program of Chemical Research on Psychochemicals, found that it was virtually impossible to "hold out" under the influence of the drug LSD. So, assuming the General had been given enough of the drug, the information should be accurate. So, we had better get the General back to the Compound, but in the meantime we had better get this information back immediately. I knew that Chuck had a radio transmission code, but first we had to get to a radio transmission area. But, first, what to do about the tripping soldiers here.

Chuck, Paul and I discussed the situation very briefly, and we decided that we could not just shoot these few soldiers. That would certainly be immoral. It would be like shoot fish in a barrel. And it would be much like the Germans shooting down paratroopers while they were still in the sky, during World War Two. We decided that the LSD trip for these souls would last for at least several hours. Enough time for us to get out of here and hopefully signal Command, and be on our way with General Diem. So, that is what we did. We put the duct tape back on the General, and he certainly didn't care much. He was definitely in La La Land. We back out through the tree line and made it back to where we had left the Jeep. This was no easy task since we had to lug the General from time to time. We took turns doing that. Once we got him into the Jeep, it would be, hopefully, home free. We needed to signal Command on a secure line using code. Chuck was adept at code, so when we established radio contact with Command, he broke into his elaborate code. It made me think of the stories of the Indian Code Whispers during World War Two.

So, we were now on our way. With the immediate crisis over for us, it gave me time to revisit my guilt. It came back with a vengeance. How would I ever be able to live with myself after what I had done? This was not supposed to happen to me. I was a non-combatant, not a killing machine.

Chuck noticed my staring out into the distance. He said, "Tommy, you had to do what you did. You have also saved untold number of lives. You are going to be put up for a medal for your valor, and not only a Purple Heart. If what you have prevented by your heroics has saved not only a single Marine, but also at least company of Marines and soldiers as well as airmen, planes and Tan Son Nhut, then by God, you are a hero. We couldn't have done it without you Tommy. You were the one who knew how to extract the information from General Diem. If I had to do it, or if Paul had to do it, we probably would have just threatened him and no doubt killed him in the process, with the information he had, being lost. Tran was a young boy, yes, but he was the enemy who was trying to kill you. Never forget that. He was trying to kill you, and if he succeeded, he could have possibly killed Pauly and me. He may not have started out that way, but he became a killing machine for the enemy, no matter how well intentioned he might have been."

I had to admit that what Chuck was telling me made some semblance of sense. I certainly didn't think I was a hero, but maybe I was in a kill or be killed situation, and maybe God would understand that, even if I didn't.

It took us several hours to get back to Command. When we pulled up to the compound within the compound, the same Marine guard was on duty. He recognized us, and this time didn't ask for any ID, and waved us through. We then approached Colonel Frey's office, and the guard on duty started to ask for ID but Colonel Frey came out and greeted us.

"Welcome back Chuck, Paul, Tom. We acted on the information you called into us. Is this General Diem? He appears to still be in the land of the bright lights. Come on in and bring the General with you. I have a couple of Marines inside. They will take him after I get a chance to chat with him, or should I say try to chat with him? The information he gave you was accurate. No sooner than we got the warning from you, we had a battalion surround Tan Son Nhut, the planes and the runways. We had this end of the Cu Chi tunnels surrounded. The assault was clearly scheduled to begin today. Apparently they didn't need to be led by General Diem. As soon as those little gooks started coming out, we let them come, and then had spot lights shine on them, blew whistles like they do when they are attacking, and fired an initial volley over their heads. The ones who shot back we had to take out, but there were not many that did that. Most of them surrendered, and we have them corralled in the Northwest section of the base. Gentlemen, you saved a hell of a lot of good men, ours and theirs. You should be proud. We are proud of you. Your country is proud of you. Chuck, I am acting on your recommendation that Tom, here, receives a "Star," along with a Purple Heart. You and Paul will both be up for a Navy Cross. You all saved lives, more than you can ever know.

Now you get some rest, a beer, or whatever. We will take it from here. I will see you here tomorrow."

General Diem was starting to come down from his psychedelic trip. He had no clue what he had divulged, but he would soon find out. He would also learn that he would revisit his visual hallucinations if he didn't come across with more information. All I knew was that I wouldn't be a part of that again. Just one more thing about which I would feel guilt. Nothing, but nothing, however would haunt me like the taking of a life. I could rationalize taking part in a drug enhanced interrogation, but killing a boy? Never.

We headed back to our quarters, again dropping Paul at the enlisted barracks. I hugged him and thanked him for stopping the bleeding and no doubt saving my life.

He merely said, "Not to worry, Bac Si. You would have done it for me. And besides, it was you who were able to get the information we needed to save more lives than just yours. And, you only did what you had to do. You had no choice Tommy. Remember that, you had absolutely no choice, understand?"

He headed into his barracks. I knew he would be able to somehow get himself a beer, maybe a Budweiser.

Chuck and I pulled away and headed towards the BOQ. He said, "Tommy, let's get a beer before we get some rack time, ok? Unless you want or need to go to the dispensary to have your wound looked at."

I said "Sure. Let's get a beer. I am sure Pauly took care of my wound well enough that it can wait until tomorrow to have someone at the dispensary look at it. Insofar as sleep is concerned, I'm not sure I can sleep anyway. Chuck, I can't get rid of the thought of Tran's face. I'm not sure I ever will."

He said, "Tom, you have to. If you don't, it will haunt you. You have to let it go. It is too fresh right now, but you have to find something or someone to help you let it go, and I don't mean another shrink. That might help, but we need someone, a special someone who will tell us that it's all right. I hope you have that special someone, and if you don't, I hope you find her."

My mind flashed to Carolyn, but then I realized she was married, and that I would never see her again. She married that Indian, and probably was a squaw with at least two little papooses.

CHAPTER 23

On Base

We decided to have a couple of beers in the Officer's Club, close to our quarters. The Club was not crowded as it was late. We sat at a table near the head, and Chuck went to the bar and got us a couple of beers, Ba Ma Ba, the "33" beer. My chest still hurt from the stab wound, and I supposed I should have had it looked at, at the dispensary, but I just didn't want to. And besides, I think Paul's suturing skills were pretty good. What else would or could the doc on call at the dispensary do, other than to tell me to keep the wound clean, and maybe give me an antibiotic. I probably would go to the dispensary before I left and get an antibiotic, since who knows what Tran had been cutting with his knife before he cut me.

I said to Chuck, "Thanks for getting me through what we went through. I really could not have made it through without you, and Paul as well. Thanks for recommending me for 'the Star,' although I don't deserve it. Chuck, I killed a kid. How am I ever going to live with that? By the way, do you still have the ID's you took from General Diem and Tran? I didn't search Tran before I left him tied up after I killed him. I don't know if he had a family picture with him, like they usually have. Like we usually have."

Chuck reached in his pocket and pulled out two North Vietnamese Identification booklets. They sort of resemble our passports. One of them was General Diem's and the other was Tran's. Tran's appeared thinner and quite frankly more worn. That was probably because he had to do more grunt work and maybe he opened and closed it more than the General did, or would have to. People would recognize General Diem, but probably not Tran so much. Tran would have probably had to show his credentials more often than the General. Chuck handed both identification booklets over to me. We both nursed our beers, and I flipped through General Diem's booklet first. Most of what was in it was name, rank and serial number stuff. Some personal data was included, like date and place of birth. There was also a picture of Ho Chi Minh on the inside cover. I guess Ho was actually "the father of his country." There were no personal pictures in the General's ID booklet. I placed that ID on the table and picked up Tran's.

I shuttered when I picked up his. It was sort of like what one hears about when some people walk by a graveyard. But now I was the one who was getting anxious. I was opening the personal history of a man I just killed. No, a boy I just killed. The inside cover had the same picture of Ho Chi Minh that was in the General's identification booklet. Then I saw his name. Tran Noc Anh. Certainly I knew his first name, but not his middle and last names. But, there was something vaguely familiar about him, his name, and well I don't know, just something. My guilt was obviously playing tricks on my judgment here? How could I possibly know this boy? I have only been in country a matter of days. Yet, there was something. I continued looking through his identification booklet. The same data was listed, as was in General Diem's booklet. Name, rank, serial number, place and date of birth. There was a picture folded in the back pocket of the booklet. I removed it and unfolded it. It was crumpled and clearly worn and suffered from being folded many times. It was a family. Clearly it was Tran's family, as I did recognize him, even though it was when he was a bit younger.

He was standing between, probably, his mother and father, and a little girl. The little girl seemed familiar to me. She was holding Tran's hand, much like a little sister would with her bigger brother. My eyes were tired but focused. I put the picture down, but then picked it up again and stared at the little girl. It was Quynh, my little patient from Bethesda. I would swear to it. But, could I. She was a bit younger in the picture, as was Tran. But her little smile. I would recognize that smile anywhere. Oh my God, I killed her brother. I dropped the picture and tried to stand up, but couldn't. Chuck asked me what was the matter. I couldn't speak. I couldn't stand. My mind was racing. What did I do? What can I do? What should I do? I tried to clear my mind. I reminded myself that I was a psychologist and that I knew how to deal with this. I knew that I could figure out what to do, or at least I said that to myself. I shook my head, like I was trying to shake the cobwebs out. Chuck asked again if I was ok.

I snapped myself out of it and said, "Yeah, sure. I'm fine."

I handed Tran's identification booklet back to Chuck, but I asked if I could hold on to the picture for a bit. He said that I could, at least for the time being. He said he wasn't sure if it would be needed, but again, that I could hold on to it for now. I guess he felt that I needed to make peace with Tran through a personal picture. I drank the rest of my beer and said to Chuck, "Hey, I'm tired. Do you mind if we go now?"

He said, "Sure," and left a couple of dollars on the table and we left.

In the Jeep, Chuck looked at me and said, "Hey Tom, are you ok? You look like you've seen a ghost. I know that seeing something personal of Tran's is upsetting you but are you ok?"

I assured him that I was, even though he clearly knew that something was up. We didn't talk during the rest of the short ride. We parked the Jeep and walked into the BOQ. He asked me again if I was ok, and I assured him that I was. He knew better, but let it slide. He said that he'd meet me in the morning at 0800, in the lobby. I nodded and went to my room. I opened the door, locked it, and turned on the light on the table next to my bed. I lay down on my bed and held up above me, the picture of Tran and his family. Could this really be my little patient or was my imagination fueled by guilt playing tricks on me? The smile on the little girl's face was unmistakably that of Quynh. I wept.

Sleep was fitful. I felt like an alcoholic because I was craving a scotch. I sat up and tried to piece together all that had transpired in the last twenty-four hours. What did I do? What did I have to do? Would I be able to live with my actions? I knew that I would have to. I knew I had enough ego strength not to be suicidal. Self-destructive maybe, but definitely not suicidal. I had to think this through. As a psychologist, sometimes you would refer someone to the Chaplin, when there seemed to be a moral or spiritual issue. Was this that time for me? Would I ever be able to tell anyone about what happened? Would I ever be able to face Quynh again? Would I ever have to? What are the chances of that encounter ever happening? I had to get some sleep. I just kept begging God to let me sleep.

Sleep was sporadic. I kept waking up, usually soaked with perspiration, and not from the humidity since my room was air-conditioned. I kept having nightmares. They were of Tran coming at me with his knife, stabbing me, and then me plunging my knife into him. The strange part of the nightmares was that Tran was thanking me. Thanking me? Why in the hell would he be thanking me? Maybe he didn't want to be there any more than I did. Did he somehow think that the little patient I told him about was his sister, Quynh? That was a stretch, but your mind can really do a number on you. And, it was my profession that was supposed to figure that stuff out.

Morning finally came. Light filtered through the shades and

filled my room. I looked at my watch. It was 0600. My fitful sleep finally ended. I never had required a lot of sleep, so this was not terribly a big problem for me, at least the functioning throughout the day part. My mind kept working, and now it added another guilt dimension. I felt, however, a bit less guilty than the night before. Perhaps it was the defense mechanism of Rationalization, again, protecting my ego from getting hurt. In that respect, Freud was right. And not everything was sexual.

I packed up my duffle bag, even though I really hadn't taken much out of it. I had taken a shower and put on a clean khaki uniform. I wasn't sure what the protocol with Colonel Frey would be this morning, but quite frankly I didn't care. What could they do, send me to Viet Nam? I checked out of the BOQ and waited outside for Chuck to find me. It was still early, so I walked around the BOQ area for a bit. I walked back into the BOQ and asked one of the Filipino stewards if they had a cup of coffee. One of them brought me a piping hot cup of coffee, and I slipped him a dollar. At first he was reluctant to take it, but I insisted. I looked up from my coffee and saw Chuck and Paul walking up. Chuck had picked up Paul before he came for me. Clearly Chuck had gotten up and out before I did. Typical Marine, never late.

"Morning Tom, sleep ok?"

I said, "Yeah sure Chuck, as well as can be expected. How about you? Pauly?"

They both said that they slept ok and that they had probably slept better than me. They seemed legitimately concerned about me. They both assured me that what I was feeling was normal. They counseled me that I shouldn't keep it in, and that I should talk about it. They knew I wasn't ready to do that. It was way too fresh. This had happened only yesterday, yet, I had to admit I was so thankful to be alive and out of the jungle, that I was not overwhelmed by guilt. Feeling guilty yes, but not overwhelmed. Maybe

I was stronger than I thought. But, that would remain to be seen. I had a life ahead of me. All I knew was that I had to get out of here. I wasn't sure if I would or could go back to the Repose. Maybe I could go back to Pearl Harbor. What I would really prefer is to finish out my tour back at Bethesda. Who was going to decide I didn't know, but if I would be asked, I would certainly make my preferences known, for whatever good that might be. All I knew was that I was going to have to meet with Colonel Frey. Thankfully I was not going to have to meet with him alone. Chuck and Paul would be there.

CHAPTER 24

Colonel Frey's Office

We were ushered into Colonel Frey's office by the Marine guard. He saluted us and held the door open as we entered. Colonel Frey stood up from behind his desk, came around and shook our hands.

"Gentlemen, mission accomplished. Your country is proud of you. I am proud of you. I have the honor of presenting you with your commendations. Chuck, you and Paul here have received commendations like these in the past. Tom, this is a first for you, and my guess is that it is the first for any psychologist in the Navy. You have saved lives, our side and theirs. Even if there weren't medals for you, humanity would be grateful. Well done."

We each thanked the Colonel, who then told us to stand easy and to sit down. He went over our mission and assured us that General Diem was cooperating with his debriefing, and without any LSD. He said that the General, as a military man, did not want to waste lives, theirs or ours. But perhaps most importantly, he was grateful that his brother was safe, and that we were taking good care of him. The General would remain in custody, and would continue to be debriefed as long as necessary. He did ask again about his aide, and appeared somewhat distraught that he had died, but knew that he was a patriot and that his death was at the hands of another patriot, only on the other side. I wondered if the Colonel was saying that for my benefit, since I was certain that he knew what torment I had been feeling. He knew that I was not combat prepared, and could only assume that because of my training, I would get through this or at least handle it. I could only hope that I would be able to, but it would be one day at a time. Now, however, much depended on where I was to be sent from here.

"Tom, Chuck is going to fly you back to the Repose, but not until after Christmas. You will be staying here and triaging the psychological problems, be it combat fatigue, malingering, or head injuries. You will be working with our Army counterparts in the dispensary in Saigon, and at Tan Son Nhut. You might have to go out to one of the MASH units, but I will try to keep you here and out of the bush. My guess is that after you are back on the Repose for a short while, working with Lieutenant Commander Rosen again, you will be sent back to CONUS, via Pearl Harbor, and then probably back to Bethesda, where you will no doubt instruct interns and residents, in battlefield psychological intervention. I doubt if you are going to have to do any interrogations back there. But that is my best guess. Once you leave my command, I will have no control over your orders. But, the brass is clearly aware of what you have accomplished out here, and I know they will act accordingly, and what is in the best interest of the Navy, and yours, of course. You are the first Silver Star of the Medical Service Corps. I am confident that BuMed will treat you well."

Christmas was less than a month away. I knew I could hack it for a month or so, and then the Repose. Hopefully I could get an R&R soon. So, before I left Colonel Frey's office I turned and asked him, "Sir, I know I haven't been in-country long enough, but is there any chance of getting an R&R anyway?"

He didn't even look up from his desk but said, "You got it, Lieutenant."

The next day I hopped a helicopter over to China Beach, and had three days sitting on warm sand and looking out onto the blue sea, trying to think about absolutely nothing. So I sat there and drank beer. For the most part, the thoughts about what I had just gone through and what I had just had to do, lessened. Only at night the dreams would come. I would try to force them out of my mind by conjuring up my memories of long, long ago. I really did have a wonderful time in college, much more than in graduate school. The memories of that special coed back then helped quelch the demons.

The R&R ended and I did feel a bit better, yet I noticed I was staring into space. As long as I was busy, I was focused, but as soon as there was nothing to occupy my periphery, I merely kept looking into the distance.

The 1000-yard stare?

I met Chuck when I returned from R&R. He asked about China Beach. He had been there for R&R, but had also been to Sydney, Australia on another, more extended one. I wouldn't be taking one of those seven day R&R's, and quite frankly I just wanted to get back to the Western Hemisphere.

My triage work at the hospital in Saigon, and at the dispensary was fairly routine. I didn't see one case of what I would have describe as malingering. I did see severe anxiety attacks, usually brought on my either fear or guilt. Head injuries would abound, with several of them being sent out to the Repose. Christmas was coming, and although we were in a war zone, there was a buzz in the air about that particular holiday. We heard that Bob Hope and his entourage would be coming to put on a show. He would be coming by helicopter. Bob Hope, with golf club in hand, would always have great looking girls in his show. Those mini-skirts would no doubt lift the spirits of all the red blooded G.I.'s

So on Christmas Day, while having to triage medevac wounded, I heard the sound of a helicopter coming in, but it was probably about one klick away. As it approached, we all looked up and saw this helicopter, painted in red. I think we all started to think that it might be

"Charlie" with some type of new chopper. We started to take cover, but someone looked up and yelled "its Santa." Unbelievable! There was Santa, in the gunner's door of the Huey helicopter, throwing bags of candy, bubble gum, boxes of cookies, and even pictures of cities back in the world. When one of the city pictures floated to the ground, my mind flashed back to Milwaukee, and again, that special coed who had captured my heart, so many years before, the one whose pictures I had carried with me even to this place, a place I would have thought that even Santa wouldn't know existed. Thinking of those special times with that special girl, way back when, helped get me through that Christmas in Viet Nam.

Two days after Christmas I got my orders. I would be heading back to Bethesda, by-passing both the Repose and Pearl Harbor. I could go out to the Repose on a helicopter, out and back, if I needed to clean up things there. Other than saying goodbye to Joel Rosen, there was no need for me to do that, so I opted to just send him word that I was going home and that maybe we could touch base when we were both back in the States. I still had my car and personal things at Pearl Harbor, but I was assured that the Navy could arrange for them to be picked up and sent to my home of record or the place from which I was ordered to active duty. In my case that was Washington, D.C. I opted for that, but would also arrange for a friend of mine at the Pearl Harbor Dispensary to sell my car whenever he could. He had a set of keys to the car, and as a friend I trusted him. I wasn't going to worry about any of that stuff. I just wanted to get home.

But, before I left Saigon, I worked a day in the dispensary, and saw a number of little Vietnamese children who were injured in an attack on their villages. When I talked to them in their native language, my Vietnamese having improved significantly during the past couple of months, they seemed to be less anxious, and as a consequence, much easier to treat for their wounds, both physical

and emotional. I carried one little boy from a stretcher to the operating area. I explained to him what was going to happen next, that
another Bac Si was going to help him fall asleep so we could make
him all better.

He was understandably still frightened and held on to me, crying
"Bac Si, Bac Si."

Then I had to leave.

CHAPTER 25

Back to "The World"

As I boarded the flight back to "The World," I waved at Chuck and Paul. They had both come to see me off. We said that we would keep in touch, but knowing probably that we wouldn't. They were good guys. They were experienced in the game of war, if one would ever be experienced in war, and if it really was a game. Nevertheless, they saved my life, and I would never forget them, even if we never saw each other again.

The flight lifted off, and I didn't want to look out, or back. I just wanted to be done with that. I loved the people, especially the little ones I met, and I would always remember the little guy who clung to me and crying "Bac Si, Bac Si," as I brought him to surgery. I knew that I would always be Bac Si.

We touched down in Pago Pago, American Samoa. We deplaned for a couple of hours, and I grabbed a beer and some taro chips. Next stop, Hickam Air Force Base, Hawaii, where we would refuel, and head off to San Francisco. At Hickam I grabbed another beer, and a burger and fries. That burger and fries yelled "America" to me. No more "pho", which was a Vietnamese soup. Although there was American food at the base in Saigon, the fact that it was cooked there made me feel that it really wasn't American food, even if it was an occasional steak and potatoes. I couldn't wait to get to San Francisco, where we would deplane once again, and this time shuttle to San Francisco International Airport, where I would catch a commercial flight back to Washington National.

An Air Force Sergeant on the flight said to me, "Sir, you might want to change out of your uniform. You might want to put on an aloha shirt or something civilian."

I thought that was odd. We were coming back to our country, having just served overseas. I knew there were anti-war protestors; they were on campus at Georgetown, when I was there. I guess I didn't put two and two together. But, we were landing at Travis Air Force Base, right outside of San Francisco. It was early evening, and my flight out of San Francisco International would be later that evening. I would have enough time to take a cab, if a shuttle wasn't available from Travis to San Francisco International. I did just that, take a cab. But, I did not heed the Sergeant's advice, and wore my uniform. Big mistake. Fortunately I was only carrying my duffle bag. As I stepped out of the taxi, a number of, shall I say, hippies, gathered around me and chanted something about "how many babies did you kill today?"

Having just held a Vietnamese child in my arms less than forty-eight hours ago, being called a "baby killer," was not what I expected to be called or how I really thought I would be greeted. No one spit on me, although I later heard that other military personnel had that happen to them. Someone did throw a wad of gum at me though. I ran into the airport, leaving the taunts behind me. I thought to myself, "If this would be happening to me back in Gary, I wouldn't be running from the problem, I would be running to it." But once I was inside the airport, although there were no "welcome home's," I felt ok. I went to the counter of World Airways, and checked in. My travel voucher worked.

The girl who checked me in smiled and did say "Welcome home Lieutenant Staffierri."

That felt good. I picked up a couple of magazines and a newspaper from one of the airport stores. I was ready to board, and couldn't wait.

TOM BELLINO

I found my seat on the plane, I settled in, and closed my eyes briefly. Once we were in the air, the stewardess came by to offer drinks. I asked her if they had "Pinch" scotch, but of course they didn't, since it is not one of the more commonly stocked scotches, so I took the next best thing, a Chevis, a double. I nursed the drink and then turned off the overhead light and tried to sleep. Sleep, once again, did not come easy. As a matter of fact, it didn't come at all. Viet Nam, and my experiences were fresh in my mind. Tran was on my mind. I turned the overhead light back on, and tried to read. That didn't work either. I walked to the back of the plane where the stewardesses generally sit between their tasks, and also on overnight flights, while most people are sleeping. I chatted with the prettiest one, although all three of them were quite pretty. Questions about what did I do in Navy, and in Viet Nam, I handled by just saying that I was a Navy Psychologist. They were based in D.C., and the one I spoke with the most gave me her name and phone number. I promised I would call her as soon as I got situated at Bethesda. I told her that I would be staying at the BOQ on the Hospital grounds until I could find an apartment. She told me that she shared an apartment in Georgetown, and that there were usually vacancies in her building. Since I went to Georgetown for graduate school, I knew the area, and even knew the building. I would check it out.

I went back to my seat and tried to close my eyes. I did doze off for a couple of hours, but it was a fitful doze. It was, however, a smooth flight. The next thing I realized, the Captain was making the announcement that we would soon be landing in D.C. I was getting anxious again, but this was in anticipation of getting home. I would have the entire day to check into the BOQ, and try to relax. I didn't have to report into the hospital until the following day. So, I took a cab from National, out to Bethesda. I asked the cabbie to take me through Georgetown. It took about an hour, and we were going against morning rush hour traffic, which in Washington is horrendous. I had the

cab drop me off at the BOQ, went in and showed my orders and registered. I spent most of the day getting my room in order. I didn't
know how long I would be staying in the BOQ, but I wanted to at least
unpack and have some sense of permanence. I also had to arrange for
a car rental, until I could buy one. That would come, however, after I
got my feet on the ground at the hospital.

The following day I checked in at the hospital, first with personnel, and then went right over to Neuropsychology. I saw most of the
old crew. Sybil, the secretary hugged me and welcomed me back. I
met with Captain Flaherty, who had recruited me into the Clinical
Psychology Program to begin with. Then I walked down to Dr. Ike
Samuelson's office. He was talking with Miss Elizabeth Hanson. They
were still the Director and Chairperson, respectively, of the program.
They stopped when they saw me and came over and shook my hand,
clasping my shoulder, welcoming me back. I could tell that they were
sincere, and were happy to see me. I knew that they no doubt heard
about, at least some, of my experiences in Nam. And, of course, they
couldn't help but notice the ribbons on my uniform, especially the one
for the Silver Star. They told me how proud they were of me. Again, I
knew they were sincere, and not just blowing smoke up my arse. We
met for lunch, and after the usual pleasantries, we talked about my
duties for the remainder of my tour at Bethesda, and probably my enlistment. They assured me that Captain Mullins would probably try to
get me to augment into the regular Navy, and make Navy Psychology
my career. I told them quite frankly that that was not going to happen. I went back to Sybil's office. She told me that Lieutenant Cheryl
Richards had always been asking about me. She was on duty today, and
would I want her to page her. I said that I would just go up to her unit
and say hello. I took the elevator up to the fifth floor, and as I go off I
saw her with a patient. She looked over, covered her mouth with her
hand, excused herself, and came over to me. Clearly she wanted to
hug me, but decorum would not let her. We walked down the hall to a

storage closet. She pulled me into the closet and kissed me and started crying. I had not kept in touch with her since I left. She asked where I was staying and I told her. She came right out and asked me if I wanted to stay with her, even until I could find my own place. I simply told her that I thought we should just take it slow and ease back into anything we had. I told her that I simply had too much baggage, and that I really needed some space to sort things out. She accepted that. I asked her if she would like to have dinner. She said yes, and she said she would pick me up at the BOQ at 1800.

The long and short of it, I moved in with her a week later. It didn't take long, however, for the demons to get in the way. I began having nightmares. Calling out in my sleep, and me waking wet from perspiration, worried her. Being a psychiatric nurse, and also working at Bethesda, she knew what the symptoms of a stress disorder were. She tried to calm me the best she could, and sometimes it would work and I could get some sleep. Our relationship was good, probably better than before. Before, it was no doubt, primarily sexual. Now, although the sex was still good, it was also very comfortable being there, at home. Yet, my issues were still my issues, and I didn't want to burden her, nor was I able to tell her what had happened in Viet Nam. I couldn't tell anyone. I knew about group therapy sessions, but there was no way I could take part in any of them. After all, I was a therapist, and had actually led several treatment groups for returning military. I was to be there for them, and not them for me. So, I kept everything to myself. I just didn't, or couldn't, talk about what happened. Often times I would be asked about the medals on my uniform. If it were up to me I wouldn't wear them, but I was required to. I would try to change the focus by saying something funny, like "Oh, I must have picked up the wrong uniform at the dry cleaners."

The months passed. I enjoyed being back at Bethesda. I was happy to be doing my work, and felt that it was not only useful, but also necessary, which is always a prerequisite for being content with your career choice. I saw patients, did evaluations, and ran a couple of re-search studies. Dr. Samuelson, and Miss Hanson treated me well. They were very kind to me. Although I was not an intern any longer, they still tried to protect me from the bureaucracy, and still were able to teach me things based on their wealth of experience. My fellow in-terns had all moved on, and so it was easier for me to stay pretty much to myself. I just really didn't want to answer questions about my rib-bons or my experiences in Viet Nam. I wanted to see children again, and after clearing it with Dr. Samuelson, Sybil started scheduling me with patients in the Child Center. There, I found, I didn't have to face my demons by listening to young men who were facing the same kinds of demons as I was. Tran dying in my arms was a memory burned into my psyche. My ego strength, however, must have been fairly strong, because life perked on. Yet, I wondered about little Quynh, and if she and her adoptive parents, Commander and Mrs. Mason, were still in the area. I resisted checking. I really wouldn't know what to do, so I forced myself not to try to check.

Cheryl and I enjoyed the spring in Washington, and each other. We walked along the Tidal Basin, when the Cherry Blossoms were in bloom. That is such a glorious sight. Washington really is a beau-tiful city.

We took weekend trips, and seemingly got closer all the time, with the exception, of course, when my nightmares were particularly animated. When they came, she would leave the bedroom and go sleep in the other room. I was on my own to fight the demons. She told me that since I was talking and yelling in Vietnamese, that there was noth-ing she could do. And, she was probably right. So, when June came around and I had decided not to stay in the Navy, although Captain Flaherty tried to get me to extend, I had to tell her that I had to leave. It was probably as bittersweet for her as it was for me. Perhaps love was there, but not enough. So, we parted.

CHAPTER 26

Life Goes On

Life, in fact, does go on. I accepted a position at the V.A. Hospital, in Washington. I became the Director of the Day Treatment Center, which was part of the Department of Psychiatry, Outpatient Clinic. I found that although I could relate to the returning veterans, and I believe established meaningful treatment modalities for many of them, especially the ones with stress related psychological problems directly related to combat, I had way too much baggage of my own from Viet Nam. So, because I had also started an evening private practice, seeing children and their parents, I phased out of the position at the V.A. and went into the full time private practice of Child Clinical Psychology. This was my niche, and must have been good at it because the referrals kept coming. I didn't have much time, or maybe it was inclination, for an active social life. I dated, and quite frankly dated a number of beautiful and successful young women, including a famous young French model, who had been on the cover of Elle.

Yet, no one could fully understand what I was fighting, especially at night. Actually Dominique, the Elle cover girl, came the closest. We often spoke, in French, and she was curious about Viet Nam, having had an uncle who had been there prior to Diem Bien Phu. I guess she remembered family stories about the French occupation there. We would go to the best French Restaurants in the city, and also occasionally went to the Vietnamese restaurants, in "Little Saigon," which was an area off Glebe Road, in Arlington, Virginia. Restaurant Dalat, which was named after the Vietnamese city where the owner was born, was our favorite. We both liked the lemon press there, which was like sweetened and pulpy lemonade. They also served 33 Beer, and some of the best Pho (soup) in town. We also both liked Maison Blanche, the French restaurant a couple of blocks from the White House. We spoke French there, but when we ate at Dalat, I used my Vietnamese, and Dominique was trying hard to learn it. We had actually met at a reception at the French Embassy. I had been on the embassy party "circuit," in that I had published articles as well as a book on advice for parents, and as a consequence, frequently made the social columns of The Washington Post, and Washingtonian Magazine. Embassy social secretaries loved that sort of publicity. I did enjoy much of the social scene, but wasn't completely comfortable because inevitably the discussion would come around to my experiences in Viet Nam. I tried to give some explanation of how it was when I was there, but I tried to evade questions about my Silver Star. I always ended the conversations with, "The guys who fought and gave it all over there deserved it more than I." I would then try to refocus discussions on Dominique's latest cover shoot. That focus was relatively easy, especially for the men in the group, in that Dominique was absolutely beautiful. And young.

Like many relationships, some good things come to an end. So did Dominique and I. We probably knew that would happen, from the beginning, but we clung to what we had for as long as we could. And, she was young. I wasn't too much older than she was, yet, I was. I was a bit hardened by Viet Nam, and what had happened there. She understood, in her young and naïve way, but again, she was young. She dealt with my nightmares better than one would expect from such a young beautiful girl. She would hold me. She would touch or kiss my shoulder to waken me from the dream. It was a wonderful instinct that she had, especially for such a young girl. Yet, I couldn't, or wouldn't open up to her. I couldn't or wouldn't talk with her about what had happened in Viet Nam. And so eventually, we too, had to move on. And so that validated my reluctance or inability to share with her what had happened. We saw each other on the embassy party circuit from time to time, with the requisite kiss on both cheeks, and "How have you been?" Finally our paths stopped crossing, and that was the end of it. I read that she was back in Paris, modeling and living with a French movie star. Good for her.

The years passed, more quickly than I realized. My practice continued being busy. I had a social worker working with me, one who focused on parents of autistic children. That was not one of my interests, so she handled those cases for me. I continued writing, and had two more books published. One of the books was based on my doctoral dissertation, dealing with stress and children, and the objective measuring of it. I didn't much like forensic work, and I loathed being called into court as an expert witness. Fortunately I was able to get out of that kind of work by setting expert witness fees so high that I was priced out of the market. I would much prefer developing a treatment plan than a forensic plan for an attorney. So, I treated children.

And more years passed.

My townhouse in Georgetown was three blocks from the university, on Prospect Street, near what would later be called "The Exorcist Steps," after a famous scene in the movie "The Exorcist." I had a great view of the Potomac River, and even The Watergate, where President Nixon would later meet his demise. I was asked to teach a couple of courses at Georgetown, in the Psychology Department. I liked teaching, although I didn't think I could, or would, want to do it full time. I would have Saturday lunch with friends, at The Tombs, a student restaurant one block off campus. It was a block away from Holy Trinity Church, where I would drop in to pray. The Jesuits had that place too, even though they had the Dahlgren Chapel on their university campus, virtually across the street. I liked that church, at least until the guitar Masses became ubiquitous. Then I started attending Holy

Rosary Church, on Third Street, Northwest. It was the Italian parish of Washington. The Mass at ten o'clock on Sunday was in Italian. Afterwards espresso and cappuccino were served, and the Italians from the Embassy, as well from the surrounding communities would gather and talk Italian, in Casa Italiana, the Italian social center immediately adjacent to the church. I enjoyed going there. But I went alone. Dominique had gone with me when we were together, and that was nice. But, that was no more.

And the years passed.

Life was good. I had everything I wanted, at least materially. I had a Porsche, a Georgetown townhouse, took great vacations to Europe and the Caribbean, primarily to St. Bart's. But, the nightmares still came. And yet, amidst all of that, memories of that special coed stayed with me. I thought of her frequently, and would fish out her pictures, the ones I carried with me half way around the world, and into hell. For the first couple of years after Viet Nam, I kept those pictures in my duffle bag. Then, when I cleaned out the bag, and donated my some of my clothes in that bag to Goodwill, I put the pictures in a drawer in my desk. But, eventually they got pushed back in the drawer and, as the saying goes, "out of sight, out of mind." But, she was never completely out of mind, but just not in the forefront. I wasn't some teenaged, moonstruck kid pining away for years over what might have been, and old college romances. It's just that the memory of that girl never completely left me. It certainly didn't interfere with other relationships, but the memories of that wonderful, and safe time, just never went away. And, quite frankly, as a psychologist, I knew that that was normal, whatever normal meant. In my duffle, I had found the only other thing I brought back with me from Viet Nam. I had taken it off when I was a Bethesda. My Montagnard bracelet. I looked at that bracelet, and memories flooded back into my mind. The Montagnards were such kind people, and their friendship bracelets given to some of the U.S. military personnel, were indeed treasures, gifts to cherish.

I placed the bracelet on my left wrist, and said to myself that I would never take it off.

One evening, while sitting at my desk, I was reading and at the same time fiddling with the bracelet on my left wrist. I then reached into the top desk drawer and pulled out the envelope that contained my treasured pictures. I stared at the beautiful and innocent young face looking back at me. My mind was full of emotion. Tran, fearing being killed, killing, guilt, and all demons that usually came at night. For the first time in a long time, I wept. I was keeping all these things inside of me, not able to share my feelings with anyone, not even in the confessional, especially not in the confessional. How could I be forgiven for what I had done? I needed to get back to those innocent years, with that innocent young girl, with whom I experienced innocent love. I wondered that night, how could I do that. I filled a Waterford tumbler with ice, and poured myself a full glass of Pinch.

Sleep came a bit easier that night. Maybe it was the Pinch, or maybe it was that I thought that I might be coming up with a plan of what I needed to do next with my life, or at least in my life. Perhaps.

Again, I tend to sleep hot. I have been told that by a number of people. People with whom I had been very close. Lovers. The perspiration, however, is definitely post Viet Nam, and no doubt a result of the demons I would fight at night. They always win. The dreams that I have. The fatal struggle with Tran. I then had a thought of my two compatriots, Chuck and Paul. Maybe I should try to contact them. Hopefully they made it out of Viet Nam. I wondered how I could find them. I also wondered how I could find Carolyn. IF, I should even try to find Carolyn. And to what avail. Ah yes, something else to keep me up at night. Surprisingly though, I did sleep a few hours straight. Sure I would wake up frequently, startled, but not as often that night. I finally awoke at my usual time, 0530. For whatever reason I continued to go by military time. I walked into the changing area in my room and got out my running clothes. My morning run generally took me down to the C&O canal, along the Potomac River, in Georgetown. My out and back run would be my usual 10K, which is slightly more than six miles. Only the die-hard runners are out at that time of the morning, and occasionally we would greet one another with a nod or wave or even a word of greeting. I always enjoyed my early morning run. It helped me start me day a bit more refreshed, since my sleep is generally fitful and not fully restful. Starting my day that early allowed me to work on my next book and articles, as well as review mental notes on the patients I would be seeing that day, beginning at 9am. And, of course, running in Washington, almost anywhere in the city, was beautiful. One simply could never tire of seeing the monuments.

My pace was a seven-minute mile. Not a great pace, but it was my pace. It got my heart rate going and just made me feel better in general. I had been running for all of my life, whether it was for training for baseball or just for the way running made me feel. The so-called "runner's high," that came occasionally, was such a treat. And, the morning was always the time I would run. The walk back to my house on Prospect Street was my cool down. I would also stop at a Starbucks, for my usual latte.

After my shower, I dressed. I typically didn't wear a shirt and tie. I generally wore a sport coat over a sweater. The kids that I would see in treatment were not so off put by my attire when I was a bit more casual than coat and tie. Even the parents like that as well. The only time I would wear a white lab coat was when I was evaluating or testing a patient in the hospital. I could walk to my office, so I didn't have to deal with the notorious Washington, D.C. commute.

I kept thinking of my last evening thoughts about contacting Chuck and or Paul, and of course, Carolyn. Should I? How would I find them? What would I say? What would be the purpose? I would have to think about it this evening. I had to get to the office. I had 7 patients scheduled. My secretary, Gale Jensen, had a cup of coffee waiting for me. I always came walking in the door at the same time. She knew me better

TOM BELLINO

than most people, having been my secretary and office manager for the past five years. She was very protective of me, and was adept at the needs of patients, referring doctors, and most importantly mine. Her husband was the Head Master of one of the exclusive private schools in suburban Alexandria, Virginia. She had two children, so was very good at greeting and making the children and their parents, who came to my office, comfortable. I had an occasional dinner at her home, and she and her husband had dinner at mine from time to time, generally around holidays. Still, other than what was on my curriculum vita, Gale didn't know much about my "ancient" history; former love interests and of course Viet Nam. She would know that I might have a date, and occasionally with whom, particularly when it might make the Washingtonian Magazine, or the Washington Post or the Washington Times social sections. She would frequently take the liberty to tell me that I needed to find "a nice girl and settle down." At times I had an urge to tell her about my lost love, from way back when, but never did. Still, I'm sure she knew that there had to have been someone special. She could never know that there definitely was, and how special.

A couple of days later, I tried to locate Chuck. I had found out that in fact he did play college football. For Navy. And he was an All-American tight end. How could I have missed that back then? So, I contacted the United States Naval Academy, at Annapolis, Maryland, but they really couldn't give out personal information on its alumni, and that included addresses. They could confirm that United States Marine Corps Major Charles Caldwell was still alive. Major? He was promoted. And, he got out of the Nam. And hopefully safe and sound. I wasn't sure exactly why I wanted to get in touch with Chuck, after all these years.

It had been over twenty years, and the war in Viet Nam ended in 1975, at least that is when America had to evacuate its Embassy in Saigon. I can still remember the pictures of the helicopters lifting off the roof of the Embassy there. The pictures of South Vietnamese civilians trying to cling to the sleds of the last helicopters to leave, hoping that they wouldn't be left there to suffer the wrath of the on-coming North Viet Nam Army, remain embedded in my memory.

So Chuck got out. Great. I knew he was from Southern California, so maybe I could check with directory assistance in the greater Los Angeles area, and maybe around Camp Pendleton, the Marine base. So I called information, and lo and behold, the second Charles Caldwell I reached was him.

"Chuck, this is Tommy Staffieri. Do you remember me? From Viet Nam, 1970 to 71."

"Of course I do Tommy. How are you? I have kept up with your work. Your books, and even your social life. I saw that you even dat-ed a French model. You made People Magazine. Are you out here? I have thought about trying to call you, but thought better of it. Didn't want to resurrect any memories from the Nam. Are you ok? What's going on?"

"I'm fine Chuck, thanks. No, nothing's wrong, at least nothing I......oh you know Chuck. What we went through on that mission. Things we did. Things I did. Have you been able to put those things to rest?"

"I'm married now, Tommy. A great wife. Two kids who are my world. No, I don't think about things we had to do. Remember that Tommy, we had to do it. Hey do you need me to fly out there? Do you need to talk? Have you ever talked with anybody about that time? Sometimes that helps. I know it helped Pauly before he died."

"Pauly died? When? How? What happened?

"Cancer, Tommy, from Agent Orange. I get checked every year. Do you get checked? If not, you should. We were all exposed to it, espe-cially where we were, around Cu Chi. If you haven't checked in with the V.A., you really should."

We chatted for about an hour. We promised that we would get together either in Los Angeles or in D.C., knowing that we probably never would. It was good talking with him, although hearing about Paul got me to thinking, and worrying. Not so much about Agent Orange, but just about everything. And he was probably right. I probably should talk with someone. But, I am a psychologist. I know what to expect in talking with shrink. I know what to do. Groups? I really couldn't do that either, even if it might be a veteran's post Viet Nam group.

I just let it go. Sure, the demons had lessened somewhat over the years, but they were still there, and they still came at night. That night, after talking with Chuck, I drank half of a new bottle of Pinch. I listened to a recording of Puccini's Madama Butterfly. The aria, "Un bel di," by Maria Callas, was particularly poignant. And once again, I thought back to my undergraduate days in Milwaukee, and my young love. I wondered if Carolyn ever thought of those days, wherever she might be, and with whomever she might be. I knew then that I had to find out. I had to find her. I took out those pictures of her in my desk drawer and stared at them for the longest time. Once again, I wept.

CHAPTER 27

My New Mission

It's a funny thing about PTSD, Post Traumatic Stress Disorder, it is always there. Maybe it doesn't surface all the time, but it is always on the periphery. I knew I was suffering from PTSD, even before it became termed PTSD, in 1980. I didn't let it disable me, but it was there. Sometimes medication can help someone with PTSD, and sometimes some event can either put it in perspective, or snap you out of it.... not really snap you out of it, but get you over the hump. Professionally, I have always believed in mental health rather than mental illness. I would much rather talk about what is right with someone, than focusing on what is wrong with them. So, it is important to not only stay positive, but also look for the possible band-aid, the one that will not only cover up the wound, but also allow it to heal.

I knew I had to talk about what had happened to me in Viet Nam, what I had done. The question was, with whom. Who could I possibly trust? Who did I really need to explain this to? Who was that important to me? The answer was clear. Carolyn. She, or at least the pictures and memories of her, got me through that time in Viet Nam, now she would have to get me through the memories of that bad time in my life. Would she? Could she? Would it be fair to her if she were in a position to do that? If she was happily married, would it be good for either of us to go down that road? I really had to sort this out. This sorting out process had to be my immediate mission. But I knew that sorting it out meant trying to find and possibly reconnect with Carolyn.

I had patients scheduled solidly throughout the week, but knew that the upcoming weekend was going to be a free one for me. I thought I would wait for the weekend to see if I could track down Carolyn. But then I thought maybe the university might have her listed as an alumni. So, I decided to call the university that day. I waited for noon, and called the Alumni Office at Marquette. I explained who I was, in that I was an alum, and quite candidly I was trying to locate an old flame, from years past. Actually the person on the other end recognized my name. I am not sure if it was because I had made People Magazine years ago, was an alumnus, and they were checking my listing as we talked, or that I was on the donor list. I had been making yearly donations to the University, usually designated for the athletic department. I was always sad that Marquette had dropped football, as had many, if not most, of the Jesuit universities. But, they always had a heck of a good basketball team, frequently getting into the NCAA tournament or the N.I.T., the National Invitational Tournament. So, I had decided early on to support the Golden Eagles, formerly known as the Marquette Warriors when I was a student.

The young woman from the Alumni Office was very helpful. She assured me that it was ok for her to give out the addresses and phone numbers of the alumni if they had submitted that information for distribution. They used it to mail issues of the quarterly magazine, as well as general information, and of course contribution solicitation mailings. So, she looked up and gave me Carolyn's address and telephone number, at least the one's on record. It turned out that Carolyn was living in Milwaukee, near the Lake, and was listed under her maiden name, Young. Her address was on Prospect Avenue, which ironically was the name of the street on which I lived in Georgetown. I wondered if I should make anything of that. Was it an omen of some sort? I dismissed that as something my mind was doing, as well as wishful thinking. Now what do I do? Do I call her? What would I say? Do I just leave things alone, and just cling to the memories? I decided that it was not just that I had carried this torch for so many years. Now it also was that somehow I felt that she might be the person who could free me from the demons. If I couldn't tell her, then there would be no one I could tell, and I would be haunted by what happened, what I did, for the rest of my life. We were always able to discuss anything with each other. Could we still? After all these years? She had shared so much of herself when we were together. But, that was so many years ago. Would she even remember me? God, I hope so.

I thought about the fact that she was going by her maiden name. What should I make of that? Was she divorced? Was she a widow? I thought of trying to call her old number again in the Rapid City, South Dakota area, but I figured that I had come this far, and so I might as well bite the bullet and call her directly. I was hoping that I wouldn't be making a fool of myself.

The time zone difference was an hour between D.C. and Milwaukee, so the time might be right. I dialed the number. On the fourth ring, she answered. She said hello. I immediately recognized her voice. It was the same little voice I last heard so many years ago. It hadn't changed. Or, was it my imagination and wishful thinking.

"Hi, Carolyn. This is Tommy Staffieri."

There was a moment of silence, and then she said, "Tommy, oh my God. Where are you? Are you alright? Oh my God, oh my God, oh my God. Tommy, how you find me? Are you ok? Where are you?"

I was at a loss for words, but I finally said, "Carolyn, I'm in Washington, D.C., and have been here since I got out of the Navy. I tried to call you when I was on my way overseas, back in 1969. I called your house in Rapid City, but was told you married. I have to tell you Carolyn, I kept those pictures of you holding your pet fox. They have been half way around the world with me, including Viet Nam. Carolyn, those pictures got me through Viet Nam. Listen, I hope I am not intruding on your life. You are probably married, but I just wanted to hear your voice."

"Oh Tommy, I am so happy. Hearing your voice, and that you are ok, and that you thought of me. I was married, but not anymore. Is there someone in your life now? I read about you in a magazine. You were with some beautiful French girl. Oh Tommy, are you happy? Why are you calling me? Are you ok?"

We went on talking for an hour. Fortunately my next patient wasn't until two in the afternoon, but quite frankly I would have cancelled all my patients that day, just to hear her voice. We talked like we had back in school. Excited, laughing, sharing, and yes, planning. I asked her if she was ok, and she said that she would like to talk with me more about her and her life since I left. I decided not to push the issue on our first phone conversation in 30 years. I asked her if I could call her either later that night or the next day. I explained to her that I had patients to see that afternoon.

She said, "Of course you can call me. You can call me anytime. Oh Tommy, I am so happy that you called. I am so happy that you thought of me. I have thought of you almost every day of my life." And so, we hung up. I was on cloud nine. But, I was now worried about her. There was something going on with her. Her health? Whatever it was, all I knew was that I would help her out of it. Help her through it. Whatever it was, I wasn't going to lose her again. Not if I could help it.

While I was seeing patients, I had my secretary Gale, check on flights out to Milwaukee, for the weekend. Just in case. I didn't tell Gale why, and besides, it just might not materialize. A lot would depend on how our next telephone conversation or conversations would go. All I knew was that I was excited, and happy, happier than I had been in a long time.

Gale was able to find flights on Friday evening and Saturday morning. I had asked her to check on the early Monday morning return flights. As I thought about it, as much as I wanted to see her as soon as possible, it might be prudent not to get there on Friday night. We really should have some time to talk and process, before we would have to be in the position of deciding sleeping arrangements. As a matter of fact, I was beginning to analyze the situation and thought that maybe I had better have a hotel arranged as a back up. I asked Gale to book me into the Pfister Hotel, for Saturday and Sunday nights. I sure hoped I wouldn't have to use the reservations there. I would get a better feel when I talked with Carolyn this evening. I was definitely planning on calling her this evening.

Gale said to me, "Tom, what's going on? Why are you going to Milwaukee? Something happening at Marquette? Have I missed something in your scheduling?"

"No, Gale, thanks. Just something personal. I'll let you know something as soon as I can. Thanks for your help. I'll let you know which flights to book, probably tomorrow."

I knew that Gale would always be there for me, and I would fill her in as much as I could, as things might unfold, if they would unfold at all. She knew not to push, and she knew I would tell her what I could, when I could.

I went back to work. I had to review my next patient's chart. The fifteen minutes between patient's wasn't just to have time to hit the head. It was primarily to review charts or return an important call from a referring doctor. The time between patients stretched from ten minutes, when I first started in practice, to fifteen minutes, much to the chagrin of the insurance companies. But, the length of my sessions is clearly defined at the beginning of the treatment plan discussed with the patient, or rather usually their parents. We have had to develop a contact form that outlined parameters of sessions, including fee, length of sessions, and notice requirements for cancellation, and because of that, we never had a problem.

I actually had four patients scheduled that afternoon. And, in spite of my excitement about finally finding and talking with Carolyn, I was able to focus my complete attention on my patients. I have always been able to block out extraneous things, including stresses, whenever I am treating patients.

After I finished seeing my patients and catching up on my notes, and returning calls, I hurried home, changed into my running clothes, and went out for another run. Clearly I was nervous about calling Carolyn later. The run helped me clear my mind. I came home, showered, put on a sweatshirt and Levis, and made a tuna salad sandwich. I wolfed it down, and poured myself a tumbler of Pinch on the rocks. It was time. I sat at my desk, took a sip of scotch and dialed her number. She answered on the second ring.

"Hello Tommy? Is that you?"

"Hi Carolyn, yes, it's me. How are you baby? Are you free to talk? Quite frankly I have been looking forward to calling and talking with you all day. It's like I am back in college."

"Me too, Tommy. I am so very happy that you found me. I have thought so many times of trying to contact you, but I always lost my nerve. I even called directory assistance in different cities, including Gary and Washington. Did I tell you that I am so happy that you found me, and that you called me? Tommy, are you ok? What prompted you to call me now, after all these years? You aren't dying are you? That just wouldn't be fair if you are dying, now that you found me and that I hear your voice. Tell me that you are ok Tommy, please."

"Bella, I am fine. I hope you are. You didn't really answer me earlier, when I asked you how you were. Carolyn, there is so much to talk about and catch up on. But, first of all I want to make sure that I am not stepping on anyone's toes here. If you are with someone I don't want to interfere or complicate anything for you. As the saying goes, we can always be friends."

"No Tommy, there is no one, and there hasn't been in a long, long time. How about you? Is there a new French model, or someone? I just couldn't go through hearing from you after all this time, and then you dropping out of my life again, because there might be someone else you were with. I just couldn't take it again Tommy."

"I promise you Carolyn, there is no one in my life, and quite frankly I am not sure there ever really was, after Marquette."

We talked on and on about things. Things we did in college. People we knew. Fraternity brothers. Sorority sisters. Old professors. Old Jesuits. We didn't talk much about relationships in our respective lives. I guess we just didn't want to delve into that while we were still relishing the new freshness of "us." The more I talked with her, the more I knew, unequivocally, that I had to see her, and soon. What she said in response to me telling her that I wanted to see her floored me.

"Oh Tommy, as much as I want to see you, I don't think it is such a good idea."

I was at a loss for words. She clearly sensed my angst, and tried to backpedal by reiterating that she really would want to see me but that maybe we should think about it more, since after all, it has been years, and we have only chatted a total of an hour or so.

If she could see me, she would see that I was sulking. But, I had no choice but to either accept that she may not really want to see me, regardless of what she said, or that I should push the envelope and not let this slip away, like I did when we were young. I chose the latter.

"Carolyn, honey, it has taken me so long to find you. You have been in my heart for all these years. I don't know if you really remember those pictures you gave me, the ones of you and your pet fox, but those pictures went with me to war, and they got me through that war. I simply cannot accept that we can't see each other. Of course, if you really don't want to, then I will have to accept that, but I sense that that is not what you feel, and that you, down deep, really want to see me. Do you?"

"Oh Tommy, of course I want to see you. It is just that I am so scared. You see, I remember everything about what we had back in school. I have carried that with me, and have compared everyone I have ever met to you, and what we had. And that includes the man I married. Yes, he was a Native American. And as you might remember, I have some Native American ancestry as well. He was such a good man, and as I told you, we had a daughter. He knew all about you, but he wasn't you. He died of a sudden heart attack. And yes, I did love him, but not in the way I loved you. I have always loved you Tommy, and I guess I always will. So, yes, I want to see you."

I told her that my secretary had found a couple of flights for this weekend if that would be good. She assured me that it would be. We didn't discuss where I would stay, so I kept the reservations at the Pfister, which is in downtown Milwaukee. And, it was not too far from her house.

"There are some other things I need to tell you Tommy. I really would like to tell you in person, if you don't mind. So, can you do me a favor and wait until this weekend?"

I said, "Of course Bella, but if you think that there is anything, anything at all, that is going to discourage me insofar as you are concerned, please know that that will never happen. And that, Bella, is a promise."

She assured me that she didn't want to discourage me because she had been loving me so long. That sure felt good to hear. I knew that I had made the right decision in trying to find her, and then calling her.

I made sure that she had my number, both at the office and my cell, and I told her that she could call me at any time. I told her that I would call her before the weekend, and give her a heads up on what time I might get to her house. I made a command decision that I would not try to get there on Friday night, so I would catch the early flight out of National, on Saturday morning. I would have Gale get me a rental car at General Billy Mitchell Field, and would drive to Carolyn's house, rather than suggesting that she come and pick me up. After all, what if we didn't recognize each other. I thought I pretty much looked the same, and she said that she weighed the same as she did in college, 120 pounds. I had actually lost about 40 pounds since college. So, it sounded like we were both in pretty good shape, especially probably in comparison to many of our classmates. But, quite frankly it didn't matter to me. I just wanted to see her. No, I needed to see her.

I had some clothes I had to have dry cleaned, including my navy blue blazer. I always traveled with a blue blazer. I wasn't sure where I might be taking Carolyn for dinner, but hopefully it might be someplace romantic. And, if it wasn't particularly romantic, then definitely Italian. I wondered if one of my favorite Italian restaurants in Milwaukee was still there. It was Mimma's, and it was on Brady Street. As a matter of fact, I remember taking Carolyn there so many years ago. If I would be staying at the Pfister, I could always take her to the restaurant there, with a wonderful view of the city. Or, maybe she would just want to stay in. We could always order a pizza, like we did in college.

The week passed slowly. Too slowly. Finally Friday night came. I went to an early dinner with some friends. These were friends from my early days in Georgetown, when I came to live there, not when I was a student. I did tell them that I was going to visit an old girlfriend the next day, and would be gone until Monday morning. Of course they wanted to know all about her. I told them what I could, without going into how important she had been throughout my life. They were excited for me, and even asked if I needed them to drive me to the airport the next morning, or to pick me up when I returned. I assured them that my flight would be much too early to have them get up to take me, and likewise to pick me up. I would simply take a cab both ways. As good of friends that they were, they were probably still somewhat relieved not to have to get up to take me to the airport by five thirty in the morning to catch a six thirty flight. My flight would get me into Milwaukee at eight am local time. By the time I would get my rental car, and stop at the nearest Starbucks, I would get to Carolyn's house by 10 am, at the latest. And that is how it went.

CHAPTER 28

Back in Milwaukee

It was strange being back in Milwaukee, the city in which I spent my happy college years, and the city I thought about when I was a half a world away. A city in which I last saw someone who was so important to me that I would carry her pictures with me not only around the world, but also throughout my life. I picked up my rental car, stopped at the Starbucks closest to the university, and off I went. After I got my coffee, I walked across the street to the new Marquette campus. When I was there it was a typical urban campus. All buildings, very old buildings, and absolutely no grass spaces. Now it was beautiful. It had new buildings, a museum, a new student union, and space, lots of space. There was a lovely quadrangle area that led to the St. Joan of Arc Chapel. That chapel, where supposedly Joan of Arc prayed, was dismantled, stone by stone in France, and reconstructed on Marquette's campus. I drained my coffee and went into the chapel for a quick visit. The docent there greeted me and showed me around. She pointed out a carved rock shelf that was cold to the touch, in contrast to the surrounding parts of the shelf. Legend had it that Joan kissed that part of the shelf, which was in front of a tabernacle holding the Holy Eucharist. I touched that space and then bowed down and kissed it. I loved being there. I loved being back on campus. And then the memories flooded back, but this time they were not of Viet Nam, but rather my time on campus, with someone very special. Someone

I carried in my heart all these past years. I always knew that I was a hopeless romantic.

After leaving the chapel, I went back to my car, and drove in the direction of the lake, Lake Michigan. I passed the War Memorial, and the relatively new Milwaukee Art Museum. The drive along the Lake is beautiful, regardless of the weather.

I found Carolyn's house, and parked the car in her driveway. I sat there, wondering what would happen next. I was so nervous. As I got out of the car, she opened her front door and ran towards me. She was beautiful. She really had not changed. Oh sure, we both had gotten older, but she was still beautiful. We didn't kiss. We simply hugged each other, and neither of us would let go. We must have stood that way for ten minutes. Neither of us said a word. We just held on. Finally we both whispered each other's names, and held the embrace.

"Oh Tommy, I am so happy you are here. Let's go inside. We can get your things later, much later."

I reached into the car and grabbed the bouquet of red roses I bought for her at a florist next to the university. I gave them to her and she began to cry. "They are beautiful, Tommy. I still have some of the pedals from the bouquet you gave me before you left. I will keep these too. Oh Tommy I've missed you."

I kissed her on the top of her head, and we held hands as we walked into her house. Once we were inside, I turned her around and kissed her fully, strongly and deeply. Our tongues met, and we did not let go of each other. Every single one of the old feelings was still there. We were still two twenty year olds, in love. Except now we were older, and we were ready. Ready? What in the hell did that mean? All I knew was that I didn't want to separate from this girl, this woman, this angel.

She placed the roses, quickly in a vase and we sat at the kitchen table and held hands. We kept looking at one another, and we were both apparently speechless in that neither of us said a word for a couple of minutes. I was the first to speak. I told her that she was beautiful, and had not changed, and that I would have recognized her anywhere. She said the same to me, without the beautiful part. We caressed each other's hands and fingers.

She then said, "Tommy why now? Are you ok? I mean I am not complaining, but why after all these years?"

I told her that it really wasn't "after all these years," in that I had thought about her more than she could ever know, and that she was always in my heart. She smiled and said, "Me too."

Then she squeezed my hands and said, "Tommy, there is something I have to tell you." I thought, Oh, Oh, here it comes. She is married again, is engaged, or going with someone, even though she told me on the phone that there was no one and hadn't been for a long time.

I said, "Carolyn Angel, you can tell me anything. What is it?"

"Tommy, I am a breast cancer survivor. And, it's back." It was my turn to squeeze her hands.

"Carolyn, tell me all about it. But, first of all, just know that I am here with you, and whatever has to be done or whatever you have to go through, I will go through it with you. I will take you to the best cancer centers in the world. I will fly us to M.D. Anderson, in Houston. We will get the best. You will have the best, capice? I am here for you angel. I am not going to let you go again."

She cried, and then began to explain to me what transpired. She had metastatic breast cancer five years previously, and had her lymph nodes removed. Now she found another lump. She did not have to have a radical mastectomy, but the radiation had taken its toll, and she really did not want to go through that again.

She then, placed my hand on her breast and said, "I still have them. I still have the 'Do you want me to?' boob."

We both smiled. As I caressed her breast, I said, "It hasn't changed. You haven't changed. And that is not the important part of you. You are the important part of you. Carolyn, I am simply not going to lose you."

We dropped the subject, and talked about other things. We talked about the fact that she did, in fact, marry the "some Indian," like I was told whenever I called her house in South Dakota, on my way to "points West." She said that he was a good guy, and was a teacher. He died of a heart attack, five years after they married. Apparently it ran in his family. She had had an occasional boyfriend, but nothing lasted for any length of time. Her daughter, Catherine, was "in her early twenties," and was working on a graduate degree at the University of Wisconsin at Madison.

I said, "Carolyn, she could have been mine."

Then she said, "Tommy, she should have been yours. She is even majoring in Modern Languages. She is so much like you. She has heard about you most of her life. She always would say that she would like, some day, to meet you. Now, it looks like she might have a chance to do so. I really hope so." She then turned the questions to me, and what I had been doing, other than dating young French models. She said that she would try to keep up with me through my writings, but that it was a bit painful for her.

I told her that I wish I had known that she had me in her heart all these years, as I did her. Then we were quiet. We simply looked at each other, wondering what to do next. I knew, once again, that I wanted to be so deep inside of her. So, I told her.

She smiled. She said, "You will be staying here tonight Tommy, right?"

I told her that I had a reservation at the Pfister, but that was made in case she wouldn't want me to stay with her.

She said, "Silly boy, of course I would want you to stay with me." So, I called the Pfister and cancelled the reservation.

I asked her if she wanted to go out for dinner that evening. She simply said that she would be happy to make something there. I told her that I didn't want her to be preparing anything, and that we could have a quick dinner, and then come back and have a bottle of wine and.......

She smiled her beautiful smile and said, "Whatever you'd like Tommy, whatever you'd like."

We spent the rest of the day holding hands, talking, hugging, and kissing. We talked about our lives, and how they were and how they had turned out so far. She had taken an early retirement from teaching. When she was diagnosed, she was taking a lot of time off of work, so she thought it would be best if she retired on disability. Currently what she had been doing was volunteer work for a Catholic relief organization, delivering food to the needy. She also had been doing some writing, and actually had a couple of articles published. She enjoyed religious spiritualism and so her writing was about that. She had an article published, about Angels. I always thought Carolyn was bright, and clearly I was right, and she still was.

That afternoon we had a glass of wine, and thought about getting ready for dinner. I had called Mimma's, a popular Italian restaurant that I used to know, and had made a reservation for 6 o'clock. Although it was Saturday night, and generally Mimma's was crowded, even at the early 6 o'clock hour. I spoke with Mimma herself, and once we talked in Italian, she said she would personally accommodate us and would make sure we would have a good table. Carolyn and I both dressed. I had taken my suitcase up to her bedroom. She told me to. And we dressed there. When I saw her in her bra and panties, I gawked. She had the same beautiful body I remembered her having back in college. She caught me staring and simply smiled.

She looked at me and said, "Hey tiger, you look pretty good."

We laughed and finished dressing, not daring to linger more. If we did, we would never make it to dinner. She wore a simple sheath dress. It was silver. How did she remember that she wore a silver dress when I first asked, "Do you want me to?" Maybe it was just chance, but I don't think so. I wore my blue blazer, button down shirt, and tan slacks. And I wore penny loafers, sans pennies. I think we both looked like college students, well maybe graduate students, or actually maybe like young faculty.

We kissed at her front door and then walked out to the car, holding hands. We held hands all the way to the restaurant. When we reached Mimma's, the valet took the car.

Mimma was at the front, greeting people. I greeted her in Italian, and she replied, "Buona sera dottore."

She showed us to a table by the front window, overlooking Brady Street. It wasn't so close to the street that people walking by would be peering in on our table, just a nice view, and clearly "high vis." Maybe she knew this was a special evening, and maybe I sort of implied that it was when I called and made the reservation with her. A flower vendor appeared, and of course I bought Carolyn a rose. Actually I bought another rose as well, and sent it over to Mimma. Carolyn and Mimma both blushed.

Carolyn kissed me on the cheek and Mimma mouthed "Grazie dottore, mille grazie."

Mimma recommended the gnocchi, and we both followed her recommendations, although since Carolyn said that she had become a vegetarian, she had the gnocchi with gorgonzola sauce. I had the more traditional, tomato sauce with just a hint of meat. We shared a bottle of Montepulciano d'Abbruzzo, and then had a homemade cannoli for dessert. Mimma sent over a couple of cordial glasses of grappa. That firey liquid made Carolyn's eyes water. She had never tasted it before. We had a delightful two hours. I paid the bill and thanked Mimma profusely, and assured her that we would be back. While we waited for the valet to bring the car, Carolyn and I stood there with our arms around each other. It was so natural. We drove home in silence, savoring the evening so far.

I helped Carolyn out of the car. She wasn't used to someone offering his hand to help her out of a car. When she commented how nice it was, I said "Naval Officer's Guide, page 93." I made that up.

When we got inside I turned her to face me, and kissed her so hard. She led me up the stairs to our bedroom and began to take off my blazer while I was trying to unzip her dress. Mission accomplished. I lifted her up in my arms and I carried her to the bed. I gently put her down on the bed and lay beside her, although half covering her with my leg. We kissed softly and gently at first, and then deeply and passionately.

When I entered her she shuttered, and cried out my name. "Tommy, I love you so much."

We made love like we did in college. It was never a "Slam, bam, thank you ma'm" kind of sex. It was always love making. And it was so again, this evening. As we lay in each other's arms, we were content. I asked her if my touching her breast caused her any discomfort or pain. She assured me that it didn't, and she kept my hand on her right breast. We fell asleep. Content. My head rested on the "Do you want me to" breast. And, that is how I woke up the next morning. For the first time in my adult life, and certainly since Viet Nam, I slept though the night. No voices, no screams, no horrible dreams, no yelling "Ca Ca Dau," and no images of Tran dying in my arms.

The following morning, she started to get out of bed to go make some coffee, but I pulled her back into bed, and we made love again. I thought to myself, "Life cannot get any better than this." She asked me if I would like coffee. I said that I would. She asked me if I liked French Press coffee and I told her that it was what I usually fixed myself on weekends. She said that since I probably was used to French things, she went out and bought a French press coffee pot. How unbelievably kind!

Before she went downstairs to the kitchen to fix it, I asked her if she would like to go to the Gesu, for Mass. Gesu was the church on campus, and the one we would walk to and from her dorm, on Sunday's, when we were on campus, unless we had to miss Mass because of a late, late night before. I guess she hadn't been to Mass in awhile, but she said that she would love that. I checked the schedule of Masses in the phone book, and we would try to catch the noon Mass. I told her that after Mass we could go have brunch at the Milwaukee Yacht Club, if she's like. I told her that I had reciprocity there, through the yacht club to which I belonged, back in the D.C. area. She liked that plan. So after coffee, we showered, together, and dressed and went to Mass.

This just felt so very right.

CHAPTER 29

The Confession

After Mass, we drove down Wisconsin Avenue, through downtown Milwaukee, past the Pfister Hotel, and the Boston Store, which was the same old department store that I remembered. We crossed the Milwaukee River, and curved around the War Memorial. We took a right into the marina, and came to the Milwaukee Yacht Club. We parked and went in. I showed them my I.D. from my club back home. They welcomed me and directed us to the dining room. It was a beautiful day overlooking the Lake. There weren't too many people at the club that day. We had the dinning room almost to ourselves. That was good, because I thought I might want to tell Carolyn about the war, about what I did in the war. But, in case the servers would hover around us, I decided it might be best to wait until we got back to her house. But, at least it sort of set the mood, in terms of her maybe not thinking I was a monster, a killer, a baby killer. I tried to put it out of my mind, and just tried to enjoy being with Carolyn, in such a beautiful setting. We had brunch, and even had a Bloody Mary. On our way out, I stopped at the souvenir and clothing concession. I bought her a hat and a coffee travel mug, both with the logo of the Milwaukee Yacht Club. I was a bit surprised that she had not been there before.

We made it back to her house, again, holding hands all the way. And again, I helped her out of the car. She really liked that and even said, "I think I could get used to this treatment."

When we got inside, we sat in her living room. It was tastefully done, with comfortable sofas and accent chairs. She turned on a few lights and also some soft music. We sat side by side on one of her sofas. At first we just sat there, neither of us speaking. I looked at her and her eyes were closed. She had a smile on her face and seemed content. But, I couldn't put this off any longer. I had to tell her. So I did.

"Carolyn, I was a Navy Psychologist, during Viet Nam. I think you knew that. I loved my internship at Bethesda, and also what I was trained to do. Things changed however, and I was asked, no, ordered to do other things, things generally not done by psychologists. I suppose I could have refused, but quite frankly I thought I needed to do my duty. I was a Naval Officer, and not only a Navy Psychologist. As you know, I was always good with languages. I studied, formally and informally, several languages, in addition to the ones I learned and knew, when we were together back in college. Since I was seeing patients coming back from Viet Nam, I began studying Vietnamese, and became fairly fluent in it. Because of that, I think, I was sent into Viet Nam. I thought I was going to be able to escape a war zone, but I received temporary orders to the Pearl Harbor Naval Shipyard Dispensary, the Mental Health Clinic there. Well, I also received another set of orders, to the Hospital Ship Repose, which was off the coast of Viet Nam, in the South China Sea. I treated a patient there, who was actually a South Vietnamese official. He had a brother who was a General in the NVA, the North Vietnamese Army. This patient told me something that, because I was a Naval Officer, and because it seemed related to possible harm to American G.I.'s, I had to tell the commanding officer of the Ship. To make a very long story short, I was then sent to Saigon, and was dispatched on a mission into the jungle, and into the end area of the tunnels of Cu Chi. Have you ever heard of the tunnels of Cu Chi?"

She said that she remember hearing about them.

"We had to locate this General and find out what he knew about a possible offensive that was being planned. It turns out that when you and I were going through the LSD era, the United States Army was doing experiments on interrogations using mind-altering drugs, including LSD. And, since my doctoral dissertation had to do with stress, and I had been evaluating stress patients in the Navy, well, I was selected to assist in those types of interrogations in the field, and specifically with the North Viet Nam General, who intelligence reported, knew of an impending attack on our troops. This General, as I said, was the brother of the South Vietnamese official patient of mine on the Repose, and so the intelligence was deemed reliable. To complicate matters, at least for me, the General's aide, it seems, might have been, no probably was, the older brother of a little Vietnamese little girl who was a patient of mine during my internship at Bethesda. How convoluted was that? After trying to get as much information as we could from the General, I thought that I might be able to get more information from that young man, boy actually, in a more humane way. It was then that I let down my guard, forgetting that he was the enemy. I thought we were being nice to each other. He was able to loosen his restraints, and then he came at me, and tried to kill me. I will never forget his words, 'Ca Ca Dau, Bac Si,' which in Vietnamese means 'I'll kill you doctor.' He stabbed me with a knife he had hidden in his boot. It was then that I stabbed him with my knife, and killed him. Carolyn, he was just a boy. He was a teenager. He was just a little boy. He was just a bit younger than you and I were when we first met. Honey, I killed him. I killed another human being. I have suffered that guilt, ever since that day. I have asked Jesus to forgive me, but I know He won't. I killed a little boy."

I began to weep again.

"So now you know the story. I wouldn't blame you if you told me to leave right now. I would understand. I have never told anyone else in the world what I have just told you. I guess maybe that is one reason why I didn't try to find you before now. I was afraid that I would have to tell you what I had done. I knew that what we had, would make me tell you what I had done. And now that I have told you, I am afraid you will send me away, out of your life. Please tell me that you forgive me, Carolyn. Please?"

The tears welled up in her eyes, and then she began sobbing. She took my head and put it to her breast. She then said the words I guess I needed to hear.

"Tommy, I know that you only did what you had to do. I saw the scar on your chest last night, from where it looked like you had been stabbed. That scar was not there when we were together in school. I would have remembered. Clearly I know that what happened had to have been in self-defense, and also that it was that horrible war. That little boy was not a little boy. He was the enemy, and he was trying to kill you. You are so good, the best person I have ever known. I have loved you ever since the first day we met on campus. You don't need my forgiveness. You don't need anyone's forgiveness. You know that Jesus knows everything, and He knows that you had no choice. You didn't willfully kill a person. You tried to save people, your young men, our young men. And you did. And the Navy gave you a medal, a Silver Star, one of the highest awards possible. They knew. And, so do I. And, so does God. Please let it go, Tommy. Let me help you let it go. Let it go for me. More importantly, let it go for you. I love you Tommy Staffieri. I always have. I always will."

I felt the weight of the world lifting off me. I simply never imagined that Carolyn's response would be so tender and loving. Oh, I had hoped so, and I knew that she was the most compassionate person I had ever known, but to accept what I had done, and loving me nevertheless. All I could do was weep.

I knew then, that I could never leave this girl again. Never. She had been a part of me for so long, certainly at least in spirit, and now I had to have her totally and completely with me, forever. It was as if nothing had changed in all the years. So, I asked her. "Carolyn, will you marry me?"

EPILOGUE

She said, "Yes." And, that night, for the second time in my adult life, and for the second night in a row, I slept through the night without the nightmares of Viet Nam, without the nightmares of what I did there, without the nightmares of Tran.

Again, my head rested on her "Do you want me to?" breast. She stroked my head as we fell asleep. The only thing I did think about, and dream about, was a life with this angel from the past, and now future.

The next morning, I was the one who got up first. I quietly got out of bed without waking her, and went downstairs to fix a pot of French press coffee. I would be happy to serve this angel breakfast in bed, every day of our lives.

But first of all I had to make a phone call. Actually a couple of phone calls. I called Gale, my secretary. I told her to cancel my patients for that day, and for the following Friday. I would be flying home on Tuesday, and I would be bringing someone with me. She was curious as to who that might be, but I told her that I would explain later.

The second call I made was to an old friend of mine, Dr. Jim Masterson, the Chief of Surgical Oncology, at The University of Texas M.D. Anderson Cancer Center, in Houston. When he got on the line, and after we exchanged a few pleasantries, I told him why I was calling. I explained what I knew about Carolyn's situation. He said for me to let him know when I could get her down there, and that he would make time to see her at any time I could get her there. I thanked him and told him I would call him within the next day or two, if that were ok with him. He assured me again that he would make time, whenever that could be. He did tell me to tell her that she should try not to read too much into the new possible lump, and that if there was a problem, he would take care of it.

I brought Carolyn a cup of coffee and a couple of pieces of rice bread toast with cashew butter. I liked serving her in bed. Then I told her what I was planning, and what I was trying to arrange. She held me, thanked me, and held me some more. We would get through this together.

I asked her to come with me back to Washington, Tuesday. She said she would love to. And so we did. We flew into Reagan National, and the sight of the Capitol and the Washington Monument, from the air was spectacular, even though I had seen it many, many times. One simply could not ever tire of that view. She had never been to Washington, and so for her, this initial view of the city, was even more awesome. She was like a little girl, looking out the window of the airplane, taking in the sights of beautiful Washington, D.C. Later, I took her to some of the monuments including the Jefferson Memorial, the Lincoln Memorial, the Washington Monument, and of course, the Wall, the Viet Nam Memorial. I had not been to the Wall in many years. I simply had not been able to go there after the first time. I told her that I had to look up a friend, one who was very important to me. She asked me if he was killed where I was. I told her that he wasn't, but that he died of wounds as a result of where we were.

I found his name. It was relatively freshly engraved on one of the center panels. HM2 Paul W. Reynolds, USN. I touched his name, and pulled my Silver Star out of my pocket, and laid it on the ground in front of his name. He deserved it more than I. I wept, and as I did, so did Carolyn. As we left the Wall, I explained to her, who he was, and what he did….for me.

The following week we flew to Houston and went to see my friend Jim Masterson, who although he was now the Chief of Surgical

Oncology, at M.D. Anderson, when I knew him in a different incarnation, he was a trauma surgeon on the Repose.

He greeted me with "Xin chao Bac Si."

I had not heard those words or had been called "Bac Si" in years. He explained to Carolyn that although there were many Bac Si's "over there," that I was the one to whom the patients and other docs referred to as, or called "Bac Si."

He ran all of the tests and did all of the examinations himself. The lump was just superficial, and definitely not cancerous, but he said that he would remove it just to be doubly sure, and to reassure us. Jim removed it that day, on an out patient basis. But, he said that as a breast cancer survivor, Carolyn should be monitored at least yearly, and that he would be happy to do that follow-up and monitoring.

We could do that. We could do a lot of things. We would do a lot of things. Together. At last.

CPSIA information can be obtained at www.ICGtesting.com
Printed in the USA
LVOW06*1439041115

461094LV00006B/67/P